Joseph Skipsey

Songs and Lyrics

Joseph Skipsey

Songs and Lyrics

ISBN/EAN: 9783744767323

Printed in Europe, USA, Canada, Australia, Japan

Cover: Foto ©Andreas Hilbeck / pixelio.de

More available books at **www.hansebooks.com**

SONGS AND LYRICS.

Many of the following verses have previously appeared; to these are added several new pieces. The object of this collection is to present what has been regarded as most characteristic of the author's work.

J. S.

SONGS AND LYRICS.

By JOSEPH SKIPSEY.

COLLECTED AND REVISED.

LONDON:

WALTER SCOTT, 24 WARWICK LANE,

PATERNOSTER ROW.

1892.

CONTENTS.

CONTENTS.

CONTENTS.

Other Poems.

Songs and Lyrics.

Willy to Jinny.

DUSKIER than the clouds that lie
    'Tween the coal-pit and the sky,
Lo, how Willy whistles by
    Right cheery from the colliree.

Duskier might the laddie be,
Save his coaxing coal-black e'e,
Nothing dark could Jinny see
    A-coming from the colliree.

O! Sleep.

O SLEEP, my little baby ; thou
  Wilt wake thy father with thy cries;
And he into the pit must go,
  Before the sun begins to rise.

He'll toil for thee the whole day long,
  And when the weary work is o'er,
He'll whistle thee a merry song,
  And drive the bogies from the door.

The Lily of the Valley.

To E. W.

THIS Lily of the Valley smells
　　Too sweet for human speech to say;
And passing beautiful those bells
　That hide their faces from the day.

It is a gem, tho' small, too rare
　For mortal hand to pluck, and twine
With any save an angel's hair;
　And that is why 'tis placed in thine.

Annie Lee.

ANNIE LEE is fair and sweet,
　　Fair and sweet to look upon ;
But Annie's heart is all deceit,
　　Therefore Annie Lee, begone !

Sweeter than a golden bell
　　Sound her winning words, each one ;—
From a fount of fraud they well ;
　　Therefore Annie Lee, begone !

In those deep blue orbs, her eyes,
　　Pity's built herself a throne ;
Pity? Guile in Pity's guise :
　　Therefore Annie Lee, begone !

Charming Annie Lee, begone !
　　Cunning Annie Lee, begone !
I'd not have thee for a world,
　　Tho' so fair to look upon.

Hey Robin.

HEY Robin, jolly Robin,
　　Tell me how thy lady doth?
Is she laughing, is she sobbing,
　Is she gay, or grave, or both?

Is she like the lark, so merry,
　Lilting in her father's hall?
Or the crow with cry a very
　Plague to each, a plague to all.

Is she like the violet breathing
　Blessings on her native place?
Or the cruel nettle scathing
　All who dare approach her grace?

Is she like the dew-drop sparkling
　When the morn peeps o'er the land?
Or the cloud above a-darkling,
　When a fearful storm's at hand?

Tut, to count the freaks of woman,
　Count the pebbles of the seas;
Rob, thy lady's not uncommon,
　Be or do she what she please!

Mary of Crofton.

AH ! a lovely jewel was Mary of Crofton,
  And now she is cold in the clay,
We think of the heart-cheering image as often
  As we pass down the old waggon way.

So endearing and winning her bearing, the cherry
  The heart of the stoic entranced ;
While yet her wee feet beat a measure as merry
  As ever by damsel was danced.

Her voice had a sweetness that only the silly
  Bit linnet to vie it might seek ;
And the rose in her hair was a daffodowndilly
  Compared with the rose on her cheek.

Sue, Bessy, and Kitty still ornament Crofton,
  And rich are the charms they display ;
But we miss the sweet image of Mary as often
  As we pass down the old waggon way.

My Merry Bird.

I HAD a merry bird
  Who sung a merry song,
And take it on my word,
  The day it was not long
In presence of my bird with its merry, merry song.

Did fortune strew my way
  With crosses, which, to bear,
Had rendered me a prey
  To sorrow or despair—
My birdie trilled its lay, and they vanished into air.

And thus went things with me,
  Till lo, with sudden sweep,
Death came across the lea
  And laid my bird asleep ;
And ever from that hour I've done naught but sigh and
  weep.

"Get up!"

"GET up!" the caller calls, "Get up!"
    And in the dead of night,
To win the bairns their bite and sup,
  I rise a weary wight.

My flannel dudden donn'd, thrice o'er
  My birds are kiss'd, and then
I with a whistle shut the door,
  I may not ope again.

The Stars are Twinkling.

THE stars are twinkling in the sky,
　　As to the pit I go;
I think not of the sheen on high,
　　But of the gloom below.

Not rest or peace, but toil and strife,
　　Do there the soul enthral;
And turn the precious cup of life
　　Into a cup of gall.

Annie.

COAL black are the tresses of Fanny;
  But never a mortal could see
The coal-coloured tresses of Annie,
  And be as a body should be.

White, white, is her forehead, and bonnie;
  And when she goes down to the well,
The beat of the footstep of Annie,
  The wrath of a tiger would quell.

Red, red, are her round cheeks and bonnie;
  And when she is knitting, her tone—
The charm of the accents of Annie,
  Would ravish the heart of a stone.

Nay, rare are her graces and many;
  But nothing whatever can be
Compared to the sweet glance of Annie,
  The glance she has given to me.

Away to the Well.

AWAY to the well lilted Annie;
  Away with her skiel to the well;
Away to the well whistled Johnnie,
  The pride and delight of the dell.

Sweet, sweet is the well; but ah, sweeter,
  The words of the silver-tongued elf;
And I counsel the youth who shall meet her,
  To keep a strict guard on himself.

Deep, deep is the well; but ah, deeper,
  The guile of the silver-tongued elf;
And the laugher she'll turn to a weeper,
  Unless he look well to himself.

'Twas thus proved the mortal to Johnnie;
  Lo, pale, now, he wanders the dell;
Pale, pale with the potion that Annie
  Had caused him to drink at the well.

Kit never Went Down.

NO, Kit never went down into Halliwell town,
  But he flung at each lover a jest,
Till he Nan the brunette on a merry eve met,
  When his pride it was put to a test.

The youth gave her a wink, she returned with a blink
  That conquered his heart and possest;
And when next he went down into Halliwell town,
  He went with a rose in his breast!

Tho' Master had Gold.

THO' master had gold and treasures untold,
　　And health were the all of my dower,
Yet my lowly lot would I barter not,
　　To vaunt of his riches and power.

His lady's too bold, a shrew and a scold,
　　And as black and as grim as a crow;
While my own wee wife's the light of my life,
　　And queen of the roses in blow!

Young Fanny.

A CHANGE hath come over young Fanny,
  The yellow-hair'd lass of the Dene—
Erewhile she look'd cosy and canny,
  But now—ah! what aileth the queen?

Erewhile she'd the bearing which blesses
  The heart of the weary and worn;
Now many a one she distresses,
  And burdens the air with her scorn.

Erewhile she was sweet as the lily,
  And mild as the lamb on the lea;
Now sour as the docken, and truly
  More fierce than a tiger is she.

Erewhile she would play with the kitten,
  Averse to contention and strife;
Now Tab on the house-top is sitting,
  And dare not come down for her life.

"What aileth the jewel?" Quoth granny;
  "What aileth the winds when they blow?
When the reason's no secret to Fanny,
  The reason we mortals may know."

Kit Clark.

M EG MILLER skipt over to Horton,
    And sang as she went like the lark;
"A pair of bright eyes hath Tim Morton;
    Yet not his the blink of Kit Clark.

      "Kit Clark is both handsome and clever;
        His eyes shine like stars in the dark;
      Has Cowpen his equal?—no, never !
        Not one is a match for Kit Clark.

"Bob Harkas hath hair crisp and curly;
    And when to his queer jokes, we hark,
Dour Doll even fails to look surly—
    Yet Bob cannot joke like Kit Clark.

"Bill Nichol can whistle so clearly,
    The dogs run around him and bark;
And Nan likes to hear him right dearly;
    Yet Bill cannot pipe like Kit Clark.

"Tom Smith like a frantic one danceth
    As down the row comes he from wark;
And Nell's tender heart he entranceth;
    Yet Tom lacks the spring of Kit Clark.

"Jos Rutter—who dresses like Rutter?
  The lad is a bit of a spark;
He puts Bella's heart in a flutter;
  Yet Jos—what is Jos to Kit Clark?

      "Kit Clark is both handsome and clever;
        His eyes shine like stars in the dark;
      Has Cowpen his equal?—no, never!
        Not one is a match for Kit Clark."

The Fatal Errand.

M Y mother bade me go. I went :
　　But beat my heart, ere I returned,
A rat-tat-tan, and what it meant
　　Too soon I to my sorrow learned.

Her errand to the youth I ran ;
　　But had she me some other bade,
I had not felt that rat-tat-tan,
　　Nor wept to think I ever had.

Her Weary Hand.

HER weary hand the needle plied,
  Her weary foot the cradle stirred,
While in the midnight hour she cried ;
  " Be-ba, my little bonny bird !

" Where never moon nor star can shine,
  By dread of danger undeterr'd,
Thy father toileth in the mine
  To win a frock for wee, wee bird.

" He while the grey-bird warbled went
  Where feather'd warbler's never heard ;
But he'll be back at dawn, content
  If all be well with wee, wee bird.

" Be-ba,—you won't ?—you little brat !
  Well I will tell him all's occurr'd :
No, no !—Bow, bow !—Hark, hark ! what's that ?
  Be-ba, my little bonny bird ! "

Mother Wept.

MOTHER wept, and father sighed ;
  With delight a-glow
Cried the lad, "To-morrow," cried,
  "To the pit I go."

Up and down the place he sped,—
  Greeted old and young ;
Far and wide the tidings spread ;
  Clapt his hands and sung.

Came his cronies ; some to gaze
  Wrapt in wonder ; some
Free with counsel ; some with praise ;
  Some with envy dumb.

"May he," many a gossip cried,
  "Be from peril kept ; "
Father hid his face and sighed,
  Mother turned and wept.

My Little Boy.

MY little boy, thy laughter
    Goes to my bosom core,
And sends me yearning after
    The days that are no more.

Adown my cheek is stealing
    A briny tear, and I—
But let no selfish feeling
    Thy infant mirth destroy.

Fill not with looks so earnest,
    Those pretty eyes of thine ;
A lot were thine the sternest,
    Couldst thou my thought divine.

There's time enough for sorrow,
    When Life's pale eve draws near ;
The lark lilts thee Good Morrow :
    Ring out thy laughter clear !

Tit-for-Tat.

" SAY, whither goes my buxom maid
      All with the coal-black e'e?"
"Before I answer that," she said,   .
   "Give ear, and answer me.

"Pray, hast thou e'er thy counsel kept?"
   "Ay, and still can," said he:
"And so can I," said she, and swept
   A-lilting o'er the lea.

The Dream.

I DREAM of thee, and o'er me glows
    The yellow moon, upon the wane,
That beam'd when—death to my repose !—
I met thee in the Haunted Lane.

Now by her light I find thee lock'd
    Within those arms to prove thee yet
The same that lured my heart and mocked,
    When in the Haunted Lane we met !

The Star and the Meteor.

DIRECTED by a little star,
 I paced towards my own loved cot,
When rushed a meteor from afar,
 And I my little guide forgot.

Bedazzled was I, and amazed,
 When out the meteor flashed, and I
Had never more my threshold paced,
 Had not that star yet gleamed on high.

Dora Dee.

THERE'S not a may in Ellerton
   By half so sweet to look upon ;
In all the country round there's none
   So sweet as Dora Dee.

The blood-red rose to passer by,
May show with pride its precious dye;
There's not a bloom can charm the eye
   Like little Dora Dee.

The linnet's self its head may rear,
And pipe a note wild, sweet, and clear;
There's not a bird can charm the ear
   Like little Dora Dee.

The lady in yon castle grand,
May knees of noble lords command;
There's not a lady in the land
   The peer of Dora Dee.

The Cold Look.

HE look'd so cold when last we met;
  He never praised my eyes of jet,
But left me here to fret and fret—
He look'd so cold when last we met.

He may not know the pain I dree;
He ever was so kind to me,
I cannot think him cruel,—yet,
He look'd so cold when last we met.

A posy, on his breast did glow;
Who put it there? I'd like to know—
Did neighbour—she? No, no!—and yet,
He look'd so cold when last we met.

I'll to the witch, and if to-night
He frown within her mirror bright,
I'll die, and then, ah, he'll regret
The look he wore when last we met!

Delightful Babe.

DELIGHTFUL babe! to still that tune,
  Ah, hush!—This very night I'll wing
The air and catch the white, white moon,
  To serve thee for a coral ring.

The stars I'll bring to ornament
  Thy lovely neck—Be-ba, be done :
What, sun and moon, and not content?
  Wouldst thou be so hadst thou the sun?

See, Essie Goes!

SEE, Essie goes!—and thou, proud rose,
   Ah, where is now thy vain delight,
When round thee swung yon bee and sung
  No beauty match'd thy beauty bright?

Adown the close—see, Essie goes;
  . And see, enchanted at the sight,
Around her swings yon bee and sings,
  Her beauty mocks thy beauty bright!

Ellerton Willy.

IF Ellerton Willy be slighted by Lilly!
  Yet others as bonny will hark to his lay;
Then why like a silly bit daffodowndilly,
  Should he droop his head, droop, and cry, well-a-way?

> Then why should pine Willy? if slighted by Lilly,
> Yet others as bonny will hark to his lay, etc.

Has Effie, a violet sweet, and a sweeter
  In Wanie's fair valley ne'er lifted its head,
Not pined hour by hour since he promised to meet her,
  And met with this music-tongued Lilly instead?

> Then why should pine Willy? etc.

Has Tibbie, the pride of the Moor, and whose glances
  Are spells that enrapture the young and the old,—
The Queen of our dancers, so finely she dances—
  Not sighed for the love at which Lilly is cold?

> Then why should pine Willy? etc.

Has Meg, at whose bearing the Hirsts are enchanted,
   And whom as a charmer the charmer respects,
Not tipt him the wink, and thrice hinted if wanted,
   She'd skip at the proffer this Lilly rejects?

.

                    Then why should pine Willy? etc.

Would Clara herself, at whose dimples and madly
   Young Robin of Uffam would dance in delight,
Not slip a red-rose in her hair and hie gladly
   To wile, could she wile, him from Lilly to-night?

      Then why should pine Willy? if slighted by Lilly,
         Yet others as bonny will hark to his lay,
      Then why like a silly bit daffodowndilly,
         Should he droop his head, droop, and cry, well-a-
            way?

Barbara Bell.

A New Song to an Old Tune.

A WAY to the pic-nic at Ryton, away
    Went off in the dawn our younkers pell-mell;
And many were bonny and many were gay,
    But sweetest of any was Barbara Bell.

    As sweet as a cherry was Barbara Bell,
        Both tricksy and merry was Barbara Bell;
    Tho' others that day were bonny and gay,
        The Queen of the charmers was Barbara Bell.

Nan Harley was there, her locks in the sun
    Did sparkle and burn, yet woful to tell,
No spoils by her long yellow tresses were won;
    The lads only hankered for Barbara Bell.

    As sweet as a cherry was Barbara Bell, etc.

Meg Wilson came up, her eyes black as jet;
    And tho' at a fair oft ruled by their spell,
Meg fail'd even one rosy apple to get;
    No pickings were there but for Barbara Bell.

    As sweet as a cherry was Barbara Bell, etc.

Nell Dowey appeared, in her dimples adorned,
  The rose of the roses was she on the Fell ;
But somehow this rose to a daffodil turn'd
  That moment she glided near Barbara Bell.

    As sweet as a cherry was Barbara Bell, etc.

The lovely and young, they danced and they sung,
  Till down came the night and darkened the dell ;
When homeward they hied—a star for their guide—
  And who was that star but Barbara Bell !

    As sweet as a cherry was Barbara Bell,
      Both tricksy and merry was Barbara Bell,
    Tho' others that day were bonny and gay,
      The Queen of the charmers was Barbara Bell.

The Butterfly.

THE butterfly from flower to flower
 The urchin chased; and, when at last,
He caught it in my lady's bower,
 He cried, "Ha, ha!" and held it fast.

Awhile he laugh'd; but soon he wept,
 When, looking at the prize he'd caught,
He found he had to ruin swept
 The very glory he had sought.

The Dewdrop.

A H, be not vain. In yon flower-bell,
As rare a pearl, did I appear,
As ever grew in ocean shell,
To dangle at a Helen's ear.

So was I till a cruel blast
Arose and swept me to the ground,
When, in the jewel of the past,
Earth but a drop of water found.

Polly and Harry.

MERRY, lark-like, merry,
    At the break of day,
Polly meeteth Harry
    Coming down the way;
And her lips, they quiver,
When her eyes discover
Smiles that speak—ah never
    Peace unto the May.

Merry, blythe and merry,
    'Neath the noontide ray,
Polly meeteth Harry
    Coming up the way;
And his accents put her
Fond heart in a flutter—
And no tongue can utter
    What her looks betray.

Merry, yet so merry,
    At the close of day,
Polly spyeth Harry
    Wooing Ely Gray!
And when this she spyeth,
Lo! her reason dieth,
And her heart rent, cryeth
    "Woe, and well-a-day!"

A Lullaby.

THRO' the dark and dreary night,
  Golden slumbers kiss thine eyes;
Sleep, and in the early light
  With a golden smile arise!
    Sleep, my baby, do not cry
    —Lulla, lulla, lullaby.

Trouble art thou? baby nay;
  Brightest star in all my sky,
Since was turned to night my day,
  And thy father—Do not cry!
    Sleep, my baby, do not cry
    —Lulla, lulla, lullaby.

The round red moon, she's sinking low,
  The wind up-tears the very roof;—
The moon may sink, the wind may blow,
  For thee, my child, I'm tempest proof.
    Sleep, my baby, do not cry
    —Lulla, lulla, lullaby.

Alas!

ALAS! the woe the high of heart,
  Seem pre-ordained to undergo,
While proud ambition hides the smart,
  And smiles delude the world below.

Their anguish, like a Sampson blind,
  Gropes on in darkness, till at length
It grasps the pillars of the mind,
  And dies a victim to its strength.

The Dreaded Frown.

WHAT, on yon noble brow a frown,
  Whereon my hopes from times of yore
Would gleam and glow? Then, tackles down,
  I sail a sea without a shore.

My beacon gone, the waves may roar,
  And dash me on the rocks and drown;
I'd hide me in the deeps before
  I'd meet yon noble woman's frown.

The Brooklet.

A LITTLE brooklet trilled a song
  As merry as the day was long,
At which a music-hater stung
To frenzy said : " I'll bind thy tongue,
And quell thy merriment :" That night,
A dam check'd babbler's song and flight ;
But blind are ever hate and spite !
And so it fell, the brook did swell—
Ah, truth to say, ere dawn of day,
Had grown a sea, unquelled would be,
And soon with ruin, down the dell,
Dashed with a fierce triumphant yell ;
And cried, " Ha, ha ! ho, ho ! oh, la !
Where now thy skill, my voice to still ?—
Ah, dost thou find that he who'd bind
The tongue e'en of a rillet, may
Be doomed to hear instead, one day,
What shall with terror seize, control,
And wring with agony his soul ?—
In very deed then, reck the rede !"
Thus roared the flood and onward swept ;
And music-hater heard and wept :
And so weep all who'd try, or long,
To render dumb the child of song.

The Stained Lily.

WHEN first the maiden fair I eyed,
    —*This world is a world of grief alone*—
A lily she held and a rose beside—
    But I was doomed her lot to moan.

The rose was gain'd and the lily was stain'd,
    —*This world is a world of grief alone*—
And from that hour her beauty waned,
    And I was left her lot to moan.

The lily was stain'd when the rose was gain'd,
    —*This world is a world of grief alone*—
And from that hour her life star waned,
    And I was left her lot to moan.

Ah, never more in my sight she'll stand
    ﹨—*This world is a world of grief alone*—
With a lily bright in her lily-white hand,
    And I am doomed her lot to moan.

The Violet and the Rose.

THE Violet invited my kiss,—
  I kiss'd it and called it my bride;
"Was ever one slighted like this?"
  Sighed the Rose as it stood by my side.

My heart ever open to grief,
  To comfort the fair one I turned;
"Of fickle ones thou art the chief!"
  Frown'd the Violet, and pouted and mourned.

Then to end all disputes, I entwined
  The love-stricken blossoms in one;
But that instant their beauty declined,
  And I wept for the deed I had done!

The Proud One's Doom.

"QUEEN PEARL'S own equal—nay,
    A fairer far am I," May Dewdrop said,
As Sol at break of day
    Did kiss the sparkler on her grass-blade bed.

"None may my charms resist!"
    "None," Sol still kissing answered, when alas!
The proud one turned to mist,
    And with her pride did into Lethe pass.

The Singer.

WHAT tho', in bleak Northumbria's mines,
   His better part of life hath flown,
A planet's shone on him, and shines,
   To Fortune's darlings seldom known ;

And while his outer lot is grim,
   His soul, with light and rapture fraught,
Oft will a carol trill, or hymn
   In deeper tones the deeper thought.

The Magic Glass.

I.

THE INNER HARP.

THE memories of moments flown,
 Into my spirit's glass assemble;
And as they enter, one by one,
 My heart-strings into music tremble.

Even as the harp, the breezelet sways,
 So thrills my heart responsive ever
Unto the thoughts of other days
 That came and went—and went forever!

2.

THE LUCKY HOUR.

THE fickle Moon has left the skies;
 But Night's blue veil with stars is sprinkled,
And every little twinkler tries
 To twinkle as he'd never twinkled.

O, now's the hour for Love to pour,
 And Beauty hear his vows supernal;
No Moon will glint of change to hint,
 And stars but hint of things eternal.

3.

THE SECRET.

THE wind comes from the west to-night;
   So sweetly on my lips he bloweth,
My heart is thrill'd, with pure delight
   From head to foot my body gloweth.

Where did the wind, the magic find
   To charm me thus? say, heart that knoweth!
"Within a rose on which he blows
   Before upon thy lips he bloweth!"

4.

THE BEE AND THE ROSE.

"YOU won't!" the Rose's accents ring;
   "I will!" the Golden Bee's are ringing;
And tho' the winds, to aid her, spring,
   Soon with the breeze-tost bloom he's swinging.

His prize secured, away he goes,
   At which anon, in rage the rarest;
"Come back, thou villain!" cries the Rose;
   "Come once more kiss me, if thou darest!"

5.

THE FAIR THIEF.

THE sweet one smiled, then swept away,
  Her raven locks behind her streaming;
My very pulse forgot to play,
  And I was left in wonder dreaming.

The Pleiads lost their lyres that night;
  And Dian lost her bow and quiver;
They'd with the damsel taken flight,
  And never have been found since—never!

6.

THE SEEN AND THE UNSEEN.

THEY cry, "How light, the heart and bright,
  From which proceed such strains of gladness;"
They can't discern the pangs that burn,
  And seek to drive the bard to madness.

From pryers vain, he hides his pain,
  And while with skill his harp he's plying,
They mark the bloom upon the tomb,
  But not the ruin in it lying!

7.

THE ECHO.

" A DIEU !" she cried, and with that cry
  Adown the star-lit valley fleeted,
And Echo from her tower on high,
  With cruel tongue, the word repeated.

"What?—Never?" cried I, yet possess'd
  Of hope, that by some sweet endeavour,
Again we'd meet our hearts at rest,
  When—"What?" cried startled Echo—"Never !"

8.

THE TWO VISIONS.

A GOLDEN sun went down to-night ;
  When lo ! a vision from the olden
Time, flashed on my inner sight,
  With smiles more tender and as golden.

My blood ran cold ; for I did know
  Another dream of equal splendour
Would follow that ; and did, but O !
  Not with the golden smiles and tender.

9.

THE RETURN.

CAN this be her? Her dark eyes show
    Two planets in the midnight heaven ;
Her cheeks the blood-red rose, her brow
    The snow upon the mountains driven ;

Her tongue a silver bell to hear,
    Ah, death when certain words are spoken !—
Can this be her? And comes the dear
    To break again the heart she's broken ?

10.

THE SYREN.

HER harp she takes, from string to string,
    Her little snowy fingers, glancing,
Into Night's ear a wild spell fling,
    And all the while my heart is dancing.

Why thus, fond heart, thus dancest thou?
    "A dream of old in memory lingers,
At thought of which I dance to know
    That mine are not the strings she fingers !"

II.

THE TOWER.

MY wee, wee fawn, you see me yawn?
        Well, I'm not much disposed to flattery;
And were I so, you rogue! you know
        You're proof against the fiercest battery.

You have an ear? of stone, my dear;
        A heart? yes, yes, of temper'd iron,
And love of self, the little elf,
        Doth with a Tower of Brass environ!

12.

THE ONE SOLACE.

I MIGHT have wish'd it otherwise;
        But yet, albeit, they were cruel—
Those thunder-clouds above her eyes,
        They very much become the jewel!

Hope fled, but Truth remain'd, and owns
        What yet this fond heart half-beguileth;
"One knows the worst on't when she frowns,
        But never when the syren smileth!"

13.

THE CLOUD.

A CLOUD the valley domes, and down
　　Yon erewhile sun-lit mountain stealeth,
And bit by bit, with one black frown,
　　The green and gold below concealeth.

Down, down it comes, and pain me numbs,
　　To think how soon yon vision splendid,
Yon one last scene of gold and green,
　　Must like my other dreams have ended.

14.

THE SONGSTRESS.

B ACK flies my soul to other years,
　　When thou that charming lay repeatest,
When smiles were only chased by tears
　　Yet sweeter far than smiles the sweetest.

Thy music ends, and where are they?
　　Those golden times by memory cherish'd?
O, syren, sing no more that lay,
　　Or sing till I like them have perish'd!

To a Startled Bird.

(On Climbing Langrhigg with some Friends, 1886.)

FLY not away, wee birdie, pray!
　　No weasels we, no evil-bringers,
Would make thee bear the pangs that tear
　　Too oft the hearts of sweetest singers.

Long may thy nest with eggs be blest,
　　And prove with these brown four, yet fountains
Of tender lays to charm the days
　　Of future climbers of the mountains.

The Fair Rower.

(*On Derwent Water*, 1886.)

SHE took the oars and rowed along
  With such a grace, the mere did waken
Into a sweet, melodious song,
  At every charming stroke was taken.

And at each sound, the hills around,
  By many a magic memory haunted,
And skies did seem with joy to gleam
  Within the mere, her strokes enchanted.

Rosa Rea.

(Suggested by a translation from the German of Uhland.)

THE sun is in the western sky
   And thro' the barley, she—
Comes she, the apple of my eye,
   The rose-cheeked Rosa Rea.

Away I slink the maid to meet,
   As if I went away,
Alone to please a pair of feet
   Resolved to go astray.

I whistle as I go, tho' what
   I cannot tell, but know
Right well my heart goes pit-a-pat
   With every note I blow.

Anon, I, silent as the path
   Whereon I tread become,
The power to blow my whistle, hath
   Ta'en wing and left me dumb.

The lark's loud lilt so bright and clear
   Is ringing in the sky ;
A dearer tune I hear—I hear
   Two little feet draw nigh.

Two feet I hear approaching near
  —Abashed I hing my head—
Two little feet a hornpipe beat,
  Or is't my heart instead?

A floweret I of scarlet dye
  Espy as on I tread;
The maid who trips this way hath lips—
  Two lips of richer red.

A floweret I, hard by espy,
  A gem of azure hue;
The maid who hies this way hath eyes—
  Two eyes of sweeter blue.

Those tiny blooms my heart might steal,
  Did not a spell profound
Now make my mortal reason reel,
  Or make the world go round.

My senses swim, my sight grows dim,
  A-near, more near her tread—
Her little feet a hornpipe beat,
  Or is't my heart instead?

Ah, do I dream? or do I now
  Within the water near,
See, with a smile for me aglow,
  The image of my dear?

Yes, in the clear bright pool a-near
  I see her smile and—See!
Till night's o'erhead, locked hand in hand
  Stand I, and Rosa Rea!

The Outcast Flower.

YOU turn in disdain from me? Ah, 'tis plain
     I'm noisome and base?
Before on my head you cruelly tread,
     Give ear to my case.

A lily-bell rare, my charms were laid bare,
     And lo! at the sight,
In a mantle of gold, a delight to behold,
     Love danced in delight.

To him I was dear—ah me! it was clear
     That nothing above,
Below, or around, on earth could be found,
     So precious to love.

That little white flower which gildeth the hour
     When March winds rave,
The snowdrop, as clear from stain might appear,
     But look'd too grave.

The crocus a-drest in her sun-given vest,
     On Spring's live mould,
To her heart's delight, might sparkle as bright,
     But look'd too bold.

No zephyr did woo a hyacinth blue,
     With bearing so fine;
No daffodil e'er did view in the mere
     A face so divine.

The tulip so gay a cheek might display
    In deeper hues dyed;
But where the sweet smell?—could any one tell?
    The dancer enjoyed?

The pink had a bloom as rich in perfume,
    To make the heart glad;
But where was the grace to rivet the gaze
    The lily-bell had?

Not even the rose, the richest that blows,
    Could Love then prefer;
And the pansy, so sweet, bowed down at her feet,
    In homage to her.

This swore Love, and, sworn, away I was torn,
    His pleasure to be;
But ere a day past away I was cast;
    He cared not for me.

Unheeded I pined, my sweets did the wind
    No longer perfume;
To vile turned the pure—the sweet turned a sour:
    Ah, such was my doom.

I'm held in disdain! but think of my pain,
    Though base to behold,
Just think ere you tread, ere you crush my poor
      head,
    Just think what I've told.

Yes and No.

WHAT "Yes," then "No"? Thou hast in haste
  The two brief fatal words reversed—
The "Yes" before the "No" misplaced,
 Or woe unto the hope I nursed !

And yet No—Yes !—Ah, now 'tis plain ;
 No—Yes—Yes !—No? It must be so :
Yes, I my hope may entertain,
 Tho' Fate itself should thunder "No !"

Not as Wont.

"WE'LL meet no more as wont!" she said ;
    And moons went by of keen regret,
Before once more beneath the shade
  We met, where we so oft had met.

Till then in Life's grim strife I'd kept
  A heart unquelled, an eye unwet ;
But now like any child I wept—
  We'd met, but not as wont we'd met.

With Loaded Dice.

WELL, thou with loaded dice hast won
    The prize for which thou long hast played ;
And I am left with heart undone,
    To mourn what gold galore outweighed.

Yet, on the heights thy feat go vaunt,
    While in the vale I rue the past ;
The thought of one dark deed will haunt
    And hurl thee at my feet at last.

The Goal.

MY golden goal lies at the end
   Of this weird lane, I'm told, and yet,
The farther on my way I wend,
  The farther from my goal I get.

Now here, now there, it bends—each bend
  The seeming prize I seek, till won,
When lo, I'm mock'd ; and mocks attend
  My steps till I'm where I begun.

The Lad of Bebside.

M Y heart is away with the lad of Bebside,
 And never can I to another be tied ;
Not, not to be titled a lord's wedded bride,
Could Jinny abandon the lad of Bebside.

He dances so clever, he whistles so fine,
He's flattered and wooed from the Blyth to the Tyne,
Yet spite of the proffers he meets far and wide,
I'm alone the beloved of the lad of Bebside.

He entered our door on the eve of the Fair,
And cracked with our folk in a manner so rare,
Next morning right early with spleen I was eyed
To link to the Fair with the lad of Bebside.

Last night at the dancing, 'mid scores of fine queans,
The eldest among them just out of her teens,
He chose me, and truly with pleasure and pride
I footed the jig with the lad of Bebside.

To wed me he's promised, and who can believe
A laddie like him can a lassie deceive?
The moon's on the wane—ere another be spied,
I'll lie in the arms of the lad of Bebside.

Meg Goldlocks.

YE'VE heard of Meg Goldlocks of Willington Dene?
  The stoniest damsel that ever was seen;
Yet, her beauty distress'd, with its splendour, the rest
Of the lasses for miles around Willington Dene.

Meek Mary of Howdon, with Robin would rove!
But once to the Dene did his merry feet move,
A-jealous of Meg's unmatched beauty, her tongue
Was turned to a bell, and a golden peal rung!

Sweet Nancy of Benton, deemed Willie her own,
Till he went to the Dene on an errand unknown;
The errand to her was apparent as day,
And the rose on her dimpled cheek withered away.

Thus matters went on around Willington Dene,
Till East came a gallant and married the quean;
That moment the rest of the lasses were blest,
And their lovers allowed to tread Willington Dene!

Lost at the Fair.

L AST night at the Fair did I lose thee, my honey—
        I hunted thee south and I hunted thee north;
I'd rather than lost thee have lost all the money
    That all the great lords in the kingdom are worth.

        Heart-sorry in worry in flurry did hurry
            Poor I, like a wild thing alost, here and there;
        When merry wee Rosy the jewel, the posy,
            And pride of her Robin, was miss'd at the Fair.

Resolved to discover the fleet-footed rover,
    My way thro' the stalls, shows, and people I wound;
But there 'mid mays many, the rarest of any,
    No image like Rose's sweet image was found.

                        Heart-sorry in worry, etc.

With glee the Inns sounded, with joyance unbounded
    Danced maiden and callant; I into them glanced;
But who was who barely I saw, tho' saw fairly
    That never a Rose with the dancers a-danced.

                        Heart-sorry in worry, etc.

In search of my honey I spent all my money,
  Then took to the road in a spirit of gloom;
When lo, with my Rosy I met, and the posy
  I kiss'd and I cuddled her all the way home.

Heart-sorry in worry in flurry did hurry
    Poor I, like a wild thing alost, here and there;
When merry-eyed Rosy the jewel, the posy,
    And pride of her Robin, was miss'd at the Fair.

The Bridal Gift.

L AST night at the Fair I met light-footed Polly
    And Nanny from Earsden and bothersome Nell ;
And deep blue-eyed Bessy and hazel-eyed Dolly ;
    But Rosy for sweetness did bear off the bell.

            Not Polly nor Dolly nor coy little Bell ;
            Not Nanny nor Fanny nor sly little Nell ;
            Not Bessy nor Jessy is loved half so well
            As Rosy the posy, ah, no !

A scarf did I buy her, with bonny lace laced and
    A gay snowy plume in her bonnet to wear ;
A wee broider'd girdle to girdle her waist and
    A comb meet to comb out her long yellow hair.

                Not Polly nor Dolly, etc.

A lovely brooch did I buy for her bosom ;
    A cream-coloured mantle, a lily-white gown ;
A garland o'er all of the pure orange blossom ;
    The ring that will make her for ever my own !

                Not Polly nor Dolly, etc.

Some gifts to my honey I bought, and had money
  Been mine, I to these had link'd castles and lands ;
And Nan, Nell and Polly, and Fan, Bell and Dolly
  Had danced in her train and obeyed her commands !

        Not Polly nor Dolly nor coy little Bell ;
        Not Nanny nor Fanny, nor sly little Nell ;
        Not Bessy nor Jessy is loved half so well
          As Rosy the posy, ah, no !

The Spell.

" L OVE'S a pleasure, love's a treasure,
　　Why the joys of love withstand?"
Alf so pleadeth, Effie heedeth . . .
　　And what ails the lily-wand?

Lighter grow her airs and lighter;
　　Glances she would shun she seeks;
Brighter burn her eyes, and brighter
　　Burns the scarlet on her cheeks.

Leaps her heart within her; cheerly
　　Smiles the earth in silence girt;
Dance the stars above, and rarely,
　　All in concord with her heart.

Redder than the rose a-blowing
　　Sinks she in her wooer's arms;
Many a mad, mad vow avowing
　　Melt they in each other's charms.

For a season vanished reason—
　　Vanished to return and view
Loved and lover, now and ever,
　　Doom'd the spell of love to rue.

Love without Hope.

THE glory of her charms I felt,
   And thro' my frame electric ran
What made my stubborn heart to melt,
   And feel as hearts of passion can ;
And from that hour, her eyes of jet,
   And every trait and every hue,
In her delightful being met,
   Pursues me and shall e'er pursue.

A vision bright, a form of light,
   She glides before my inner eyes ;
And tho' anear she doth appear,
   In vain for her my bosom sighs ;
In vain, in vain, and woe and pain
   Are mine—and woe and pain alone—
Another's arms must fold those charms,
   Which I would give a world to own.

Upon the block with nerve of rock,
   This hour would see my head reclined,
Could this but show o'er all below
   My image in her heart were shrined ;
Yes, yes, for this unequalled bliss,
   Upon the wings of rapture borne,
My soul would cleave the air and leave
   Her mortal bonds asunder torn !

A niche possessed within her breast,
  Ay, more than life I'd value that;
What were it then, could I but strain
  Her to my heart my own? ay, what?
Entranced I feel,—my senses reel,—
  Up in a fiery whirlwind caught
Away, they fly and leave me, ay,
  Half frantic at the very thought.

What would I have, what do I crave?
  What were a sin for me to touch!—
Yon radiant star that beams from far,
  Her lustre equals many such;
She's past compare a jewel rare,
  Of value more than crowns can boast;
Whilst I who sigh—ah what am I?
  A wretch who merits scorn at most.

Far, far above my worth and love
  Is she—and were she less divine,
Another's arms would fold her charms,
  And I were destined still to pine;
Thus double doomed to be consumed
  By passion's raging fires, I know
On earth a hell as fierce and fell,
  As aught a future state could show.

Alas ! alas ! we seldom love
    Where love may equal love obtain ;
Our idols in our fancy move,
    Fleet phantoms we may chase in vain ;
We either love what's little worth,
    And live to rue the sequel, or,
What never can be ours on earth,
    And so must evermore deplore !

The Dance.

MET we in the festal hall,
  Met—our feelings blended !
Love alone shall lead the ball,
  Truth alone shall end it.

Wakes an air, and here and there,
  Soon the dance we tread, when
Ladies bright admire the knight,
  Gallant knights the maiden.

Here and there, an envied pair
  Mid the bright we shimmer;
Cheer right rare responds to cheer,
  Brimmer clinks with brimmer.

Dance we still, and dance we till
  On our vision waneth
Every light that gilds the night,
  And love in triumph reigneth.

Praised by all we left the hall,
  But, within us ever,
Rapture's self still lead a ball
  Peace should end—ah ! never.

Lo, a Fairy.

LO, a fairy on a day
    Came and bore my heart away;
But as she secured her prize,
Sweetest smiles illumed her eyes.
  And, hey, lerry O !

From that moment my career
Lay thro' dells and dingles, where
Pleasure blossom'd out of pain—
Where Joy sang her golden strain,
  Hey, hey, lerry O !

The Oracle.

LO, the vision will vanish for ever,
    That gildeth this moment thy track;
And in vain were the noblest endeavour
    To call the enchantment back.

Yet pine not; a balm—an ovation
    Is thine in the thought, that the day
Will come when thy bleak desolation
    Will pass like thy vision away!

The Rose of the Roses.

O THE rose, of the roses the glory,
    He placed in my bosom ; and O !
The heart-thrilling story, the story
    He pour'd in my ear long ago.

Tho' yet by the dark feeling haunted,
    They were but a lure to a net
To ruin the heart they enchanted,
    Their magic I'll never forget !

The Lethal Dart.

I TREMBLE like a wind-blown leaf;
  What then? I've said the word I've said;
And what if he in pain and grief
  Should pine and pine till he be dead?

My pride is victor o'er his pride;
  And then—ah, yes! the dart I sped;
Now in its victim's heart-blood dyed,
  Returns to strike the striker dead!

The Time Hath Been.

THE time hath been when they have laugh'd
    And danced, like them she laugh'd and danced ;
That was ere his sweet vows she quaft,
    And wore the wreath, her heart entranced.

Those vows she proved a poison'd draught ;
    That wreath a poison'd anadem ;
And next when danced the rest and laugh'd,
    She laugh'd and danced—but not like them.

The Elf.

IF thou wilt persist to ponder
  On the phantom fled,
Can there be a moment's wonder
  Thou art ill bested?

She who, robed in green so meetly,
  Blink'd on thee and smiled,
Fleetly came and went as fleetly—
  Was no mortal child.

She who sung to thee so sweetly,
  And to airs so wild,
Featly danced, still danced so featly—
  Was no mortal child.

Dream not on her tresses yellow;
  Elf yet only can
Be to elf a fitting fellow,
  Not to mortal man !

Little Anna.

LITTLE Anna, young and fair,
　　How with heart a-dancing,
I descry her image rare,
　　O'er the footway glancing ;
Ah, those locks of dusky hue !
　　Ah, those eyes that twinkle !
Now I laugh their sheen to view,
　　Now my tears down trinkle.

When I see her bonny blink,
　　I'm upraised to heaven ;
When upon her ways I think,
　　From myself I'm driven ;
Not a bit of use am I,
　　Save, with arms a-kimbo,
Thus to sit and thus to sigh,
　　A very wretch in limbo.

Up, from tossings, to and fro,
　　Bite or sup unheeded,
Up from bed to work I go,
　　Long before 'tis needed ;
But a-pit, love a-smit,
　　Do all I can do, now,
Still a-wry the pick will fly,
　　And no coal will hew, now.

Can it be her voice I hear,
　When my pick is swinging?
When her tongue attracts the ear,
　Golden bells are ringing ;
Do I dream? or is't her e'en
　Yonder nook adorning?
Blacker than the coal, their sheen
　Mocks the coal a-burning !

Ah, those locks, and ah, those eyes,
　Ah, the rest they've broken !
But in vain their victim tries,
　Love can ne'er be spoken ;
Man may fathom ocean—say
　The reason of its motion ;
But love's magic never ! nay,
　'Tis deeper than the ocean.

Cruel Anna.

LITTLE Anna, cruel elf,
  Spite of all my reason,
She yet puts me from myself
  In and out of season ;
Ah, the may, ah, the fay,
  Glee to mischief wedded !
Foe to rest, she's a pest,
  And always to be dreaded !

Never goes the sun around,
  But upon me stealing,
She, she doth my soul confound,
  Sends my reason reeling ;
Gars me sing, and while, alack,
  I in glee am singing,
On me turns and in a crack,
  Gives my ear a-wringing.

Pat she comes and goes, the wasp !
  Back anon she hummeth ;
Round my neck her hands to clasp,
  That to do she cometh ;
So she leads me to suppose
  By her air entrancing,
Till I'm twitted by the nose
  And again sent dancing.

Ear or nose, or wrung or stung,
  'Tween a thumb and finger,
How to be avenged now long
  Lost in doubt I linger ;
Then when I resolved at last
  Rush her pride to humble ;
Lo, o'er me a glamour cast,
  O'er the stools I tumble.

Head a-turned, heart a-burned,
  Nay, reduced to cinders ;
Nose a-stung, ears a-wrung,
  Shins all sent to flinders ;
Pale and thin, bone and skin—
  I'm a spectre merely ;
And he who'd play my part might say
  He'd bought his whistle dearly.

The Slippers.

TWO slippers in the morning red
  Along the footway flew;
Two slippers down the burnside sped,
  And lo, a sight to view!

Yon loath'd way now is my delight,
  And what was long and rough,
Is now as smooth as velvet quite,
  And far from long enough.

Yon bur, whose rudeness only earn'd
  From me a grunt or so,
Is to a golden lily turn'd,
  To charm me as I go.

Yon pebble, late but fit for feet
  To kick into the air,
Is now to me a jewel, meet
  For any queen to wear.

Yon runnel that was only heard
  A dreary noise to make,
Now pipes as sweetly as a bird,
  And pipes so for my sake!

"La, how comes this?" That question—Tut!
  Who, who can answer? Who?
Go, put it to the slippers, put!
  That down the footway flew.

6

The Fairies' Adieu.

OUR revels now are ended, so good-night, so good-night,
   And each unto our chamber let us hie,
And there lose ourselves in visions till the broad daylight
   Again has bid adieu unto the sky.
         So good-bye
      Till day has gone out of the sky.

"My couch is in the daisy with its golden, golden eye ;"
   "And mine is in the violet, sweet and pure ;"
"And mine the modest blue bell, beneath whose canopy
   I dream away the angry day secure."
         So good-bye
      Till day has gone out of the sky.

But when the day's departed, upstarting from our dreams,
   We'll gather in a ring upon the green,
And there dance till night's enraptured, and the pale moon
      seems
   To mourn the fate that changeth such a scene !
         So good-bye
      Till day has gone out of the sky.

The Minstrel.

AH, deem not when thy minstrel tunes
　　His harp to hours and glories vanished,
His star of stars, his moon of moons,
　　Can ever from his heart be banish'd.

Each tune he wakes, each note that takes
　　And charms the heart, Love's arrow woundeth,
But flows from strings she only rings,
　　And from a Deep she only soundeth.

Daffodil and Daisy.

ADORNED in many a gem this morn,
  A daffodil without a peer,
I reared my head, and treat with scorn
  A one-pearl-gifted daisy near.

That very hour, lo ! wind-a-rock'd,
  Was I left gemless evermore ;
Nay, made to envy what I'd mock'd,
  That one sweet pearl the daisy wore.

The Moth.

TO-NIGHT a gilded moth took wing,
  And round-a-round yon wax-light flew;
And, while his flight did her enring,
  He nearer to the dazzler drew.

"So fair art thou," he cried, "to view,
  I'd die upon thy lips to feed;"
And so must snatch a kiss and rue—
  Ah, he was murder'd for the deed!

The Toast.

I 'M as loyal a subject as Britain can boast ;
   Our Queen she is gracious, and gentle, and wise ;
But another this moment demandeth my toast,—
   'Tis Annie, the lass with the two hazel eyes.

The hair of my idol's a stream of delight,
   The lustre thereof with the aerolite vies ;
Her dimpled cheeks apples, the pure red and white ;
   But those are outshone by her two hazel eyes.

Her breasts are two hillocks of new-driven snow,
   Between them a dell of enchantment lies,
Where love lurks, the elf ! with his quiver and bow ;
   But these lack the charm of her two hazel eyes.

The golden-eyed lily but faintly displays
   The grace of her form, her demeanour, and guise ;
A jewel is she in heart, language, and ways ;
   But nothing can equal her two hazel eyes.

I'm as loyal a subject as Britain can boast ;
   Victoria's gentle, and gracious, and wise ;
But another this moment demandeth my toast,—
   I drink to the lass with the two hazel eyes.

Two Hazel Eyes.

WAS ever a bard in such pitiful plight?
 Was ever such seen by yon stars in the skies?
A-pit or a-bed, by day and by night,
 I'm plagued by the magic of two hazel eyes.

A leaf in a whirlwind, I'm sent to and fro,
 And peace, panic-stricken, my bosom still flies;
For rest I implore, but my portion below
 Is the rest-killing magic of two hazel eyes.

The world it goes up, and the world it goes down,
 And the lofty descend, and the lowly arise;
But fortune, the jilter, may smile or may frown,
 I feel but the magic of two hazel eyes.

Once blithe as a linnet I lilted my lay,
 And won the applause of both foolish and wise—
Now deaf, dumb, derided, I go on my way,
 Bewitched by the magic of two hazel eyes.

O Annie, wouldst thou but look down on my plight,
 And pity my case, and no longer despise,
I'd dance in delight, I'd sing day and night,
 And the theme of my lays be thy two hazel eyes!

My Shoulder You Pat!

MY shoulder you pat! What would you be at?
  A bee's in your bonnet I think!
Away, goose, away! if Flit-a-Flirt may,
  Am I to be had at a wink?

There's many a youth the picture of truth,
  As hollow at heart as a pan;
And you—Well, take one, you rook, and begone!
  But another kiss steal, if you can!

What, to Nowhere?

" WHAT, to Nowhere? ho, ho! that's to where I too go—
        What a Happy-go-Lucky am I,
    Such a pearl to have found for my natal place bound!
        —Well, just leap up behind and let's fly!"

" La! proceed, sir, proceed; you are bound on a steed
        That will fly other-where than Nowhere;
    Ah, you ride, need I tell, to a dark nook in—Well,
        Let me wish you a swift journey there!"

The Kitten.

MISFORTUNE is a kitten, clearly
  Too fond of merriment, and will
Oft love, in her mad humour, dearly
  To plague the wretch she means to kill.

She'll seize him—pat—let go—and flatter
  His heart with hope, till lo ! 'tis found
She'd only meant that hope to scatter—
  His hope and life at one fell bound.

The Darling.

M ISFORTUNE is a darling, ever
　　Most faithful to the minstrel race ;
Let low-bred wretches shun them, never
　Yet acted she a part so base.

True, oft by her the bard discovers
　He's stript of all he once possest ;
But then, just like your sculpture-lovers,
　She likes her idols naked, best.

The Breezelet.

CRIED Ciss to the breeze, as under the trees,
   She lay at her ease, one day,
"From thy rovings cease, and a maiden to please,
   Of thy doings, breeze, now say!"

"Be it so," sang he; "from the west I be,
   And wherever in glee I rove,
In lane or on lea, with the blooms I'm free,
   And they—ever me—they love.

"The primrose that well may tremble when yell
   The north winds fell, I press,
When lured by my spell, she peers from her cell,
   With a smile the dell to bless.

"The violet meek in her velvet sleek,
   In love with the freak, alway,
To my fancy weak appeareth to seek,
   When I play with her cheek, more play.

"The daisy a-drest in her blood-laced vest,
   In her deep green nest, I know,
When her lips I've prest, with a pleasure blest,
   Is her little breast a-glow.

"The glad daffodil oft dances her fill,
　As under the hill glide I,
And her pearly tears spill down into the rill,
　That yet with a trill leaps by.

"See, a fairy bold, her vesture of gold,
　The crocus unfold, in mirth,
And glories untold, where I've kist the mold
　Illumine the cold, cold earth."

Thus sang the breeze a maiden to please,
　And Ciss in the trees, that night,
To rapture a prey sang Robin the lay,
　When a kiss did the may requite.

The Seaton Terrace Lass.

MY love at Seaton Terrace dwells,
  A hale and hearty wight,
Who lilts away the summer day,
  Also the winter night;
The merriest bird with rapture stirr'd,
  Could never yet surpass
The melody awaken'd by
  The Seaton Terrace lass!

    Her like is not in hall or cot;
      And you would vainly pass
    From Tweed to Wear for one to peer
    The Seaton Terrace lass.

She's graceful as a lily-wand,
  Right modest too is she,
And then ye'll search in vain the land
  To find a busier bee;
Like silver clear her iron gear,
  Like burnished gold, the brass—
For tidiness there's none to peer
  The Seaton Terrace lass.

    Her like is not, etc.

She'll knit or sew, she'll bake or brew—
  She'll wash the clothes so clean,
The very daisy pales beside
  Her linen on the green ;
Then what she'll do, with ease she'll do,
  And still her manner has
A charm would gar a stoic woo
  The Seaton Terrace lass.

    Her like is not, etc.

When day is past and night at last
  Begins to cloud the dell,
She'll take her skiel and out she'll steal,
  And meet me at the well ;
Then, oh ! how fleet the moments sweet—
  Yet fleeter shall they pass,
That night the Bebside laddie weds
  The Seaton Terrace lass.

    Her like is not in hall or cot,
      And vainly would you pass
    From Tweed to Wear for one to peer
      The Seaton Terrace lass.

Lotty Hay.

A S I came down from Earsdon Town,
    Upon an Easter day,
Whom did I meet but she, the sweet,
    The blue-eyed Lotty Hay.

A crimson blush her cheek did flush,
    Nor sin did that betray;
The pearl is sure a jewel pure,
    And so is Lotty Hay.

All evil flees her heart, yet she's
    To Slander oft a prey,
And words of ill do nearly kill
    The lowly Lotty Hay.

Some deem her proud; in speech aloud
    Some other yet will say
She's cold or fierce, and all to pierce
    The heart of Lotty Hay.

Proud?—She's not proud: to-day I view'd
    A lammie near her stray,
And that wee thing kind blinks did bring
    From soft-eyed Lotty Hay.

Fierce?—She's not fierce; a fly did pierce—
  Once pierce her wee hand, nay
And made her cry, yet that bad fly
  Was spared by Lotty Hay.

Not proud nor bold, not fierce nor cold,
  But meek, kind, mild alway—
A soul of light did meet my sight
  As I pass'd Lotty Hay.

Upon her way so went the may,
  And light as any fay,
Or thistle-down by breezes blown,
  Went wee, wee Lotty Hay.

In cotton gown she tript to town,
  And not a lady gay
In satin drest could be more blest
  Than little Lotty Hay.

The Golden Bowl.

I.

THE BOWL.

JUST let the Owl of Evil howl !
  To mourners of each rank and station,
I cry, Come, troll the Golden Bowl,
  And quaff with me a deep potation !

Each sparkling droplet to the soul
  Will yield o'er Care a bright ovation ;
Then seize and troll the Golden Bowl,
  That beams—in my imagination !

2.

HAG NIGHT.

LA, what a night ! The hag has sworn,
  In hue to prove a chimla sweeper :
And did the North not blow his horn,
  No star would dare to show its peeper.

How black her look !—(Just like the rook
  That on my idol's brow appeareth,
When quite o'ercome with wrath she's dumb,
  And not a blink her booby cheereth !)

3.

UNCOUTH THINGS.

" I HATE outlandish things, and own
        I've little liking for the sonnet ;
'Tis for a lazy Muse, and one
    Who hath a bumler in her bonnet.

"'Tis a humdrum song, and tho' not long,
    I'd sooner be a kitten, sooner,
And ' Mew !' cry ' Mew !' than listen to
    The ordinary sonnet crooner !"

4.

TOO TRUE.

TRUTH'S words are oft so very true—
        And always when my lips he uses,
His foes, which, let us hope, are few,
    Declare he but the truth abuses.

Thus when he spake of Ella's tongue,
    She knew he meant the tongue of Fable ;
And when of her sweet deeds he sung,—
    She kick'd his shins beneath the table.

5.

EXTREME KINDNESS.

WHEN I would laugh a little at
    The follies that in Life aboundeth,
What ails the saint I worship, that
    She with a frown my spirit woundeth?

Is laughter sin? ah, then full well
    I see she'd here but curb my laughter,
And steep me in the heart of hell,
    To save me from its lips hereafter.

6.

STEEDS AND THEIR RIDERS.

DON'T spur us so: you'll ever find,
    When you will ride at giddy paces,
There's always something in the wind,
    At which ere long you'll twist your faces.

What, we're but steeds whom no one recks?
    Then spur us till we're sores all over:
The sooner you have smash'd your necks,
    The sooner we'll have gone to clover!

7.

THE WITCH-GLASS.

A SYREN, with her mirror bright,
His ear enchants; and while he listens,
His image on his dazzled sight,
A very jewel gleams and glistens.

Ah, could he peer into yon brook,
Or into any heart that knows him,
He'd find the thing that met his look
Was not the pearl the Witch-Glass shows him!

8.

NOT THE BIRD.

HE'S not the bird I took him for—
I heard him in the distance screaming,
And tho' his voice was harsh, that hour,
I dream'd of glories, golden, gleaming!

This hour he meets my closer view;
And tho' he cuts as big a swagger,
I find a little cockatoo,
And not a peacock, in the bragger!

9.

DAME MALICE.

DAME MALICE reigns the Queen of hags;
    With wink and whisper, nod and chatter,
She trots along, and never fags,
    While she has scandal-seeds to scatter.

Then when her seeds are poison-weeds,
    That choke the corn and spoil the labours
Of king or clown, her feats to crown,
    She'll dance a reelet with her neighbours!

10.

RUMOUR.

ELF RUMOUR? Ay, the airy fay
    That treads the air unseen by any;
From town to town her bugle's blown,
    And merry are her pranks, and many.

Her news our ears now charm, our fears
    Now stir, as with a clap of thunder,
And while we cry out, What? she'll fly,
    With Laughter at her heels, and Wonder.

II.

THE CRITICS.

I LIKE the darling critics—like?
  O, how upon their work I linger,
When they their weapons use to strike,
  Not me, but some less happy singer.

The treasure of their venom-bags
  So finely on the bard's expended,
One half-forgets the little wags
  Were from a scorpion-race descended!

12.

THE PETITION.

DEAR critics, pray, what have I done
  That thus you frown so? tell me truly?
"You've for your neck a halter spun,
  In blaming of our race unduly!"

Don't hang me, pray!—Just praise my lay,
  And I will swear the Muse but garbled
My sweet intent; and what was meant
  Was not the blame the Gipsy warbled!

13.

JUST THE WAY.

WAS ever wretch in such a plight?
　　I scramble on I know not whither!
The witches are abroad to-night;
　　Some wicked one has led me hither!

"That's just like you, you'll have your cue,
　　And when hood-wink'd you kiss the ditches,
Your hair you tear! your Muse forswear!
　　And blame and ban the wicked witches!"

14.

JUST SO.

JUST let the Owl of Evil howl!
　　To mourners of each rank and station,
I cry, Come, troll the Golden Bowl,
　　And quaff with me a deep potation!

Each sparkling droplet to the soul
　　Will yield o'er Care a bright ovation;
Then seize and troll the Golden Bowl,
　　That beams—in my imagination!

The Merry Bee.

A GOLDEN bee a-cometh
   O'er the mere, glassy mere,
And a merry tale he hummeth .
   In my ear.

How he seized and kist a blossom,
  From its tree, thorny tree,
Pluck'd and placed in Annie's bosom,
   Hums the bee !

The Wilted Leaf.

WILTED is the leaf, and blown
        By the cold wind up and down,
That beheld thy promise fair,
Maiden with the dark-brown hair !

Shatter'd is this heart, and hurl'd
By its grief-storm thro' the world,
Since it won that promise rare,
Maiden with the dark-brown hair.

The Charmer.

A SONG in devotion I sing to my Annie—
  Ah ! be startled not to discover I long
To fold in my arms and possess what so many
  And many a time is the theme of my song.

My manhood's dissolved at the sight of thy beauty,
  And while heart can feel and such beauty is known,
What youth could be kept by a mere sense of duty
  From yearning to call the enchanter his own?

The saint he may blame—so to do is the fashion—
  And carp at my feelings and call them a sin ;
Could beauty like thine be the price of his passion,
  He'd rush to perdition the jewel to win.

To view thy locks blacker than coal and thy glances ;
  To hear thy voice, sweetest of music—ay, ay—
Thy manifold beauty my spirit entrances,
  And reason deserts me when Annie is nigh !

The Question.

WHAT can he ail? I hear them ask;
    And what can make his cheek so pale?
Ah, that to answer were a task
    For which no effort could avail;
To say I love were but to say
    What many another might as well,
Who never felt the cruel sway
    Which makes my heart with sorrow swell.

Dear are the pains of love and sweet,
    Yet he who loves, and loves in vain,
Endures a torment more complete
    Than any love-unsweetened pain,
Nay, keener than the savage fangs
    Which limb from limb their victim tear,
And much more cruel are the pangs
    Which drive a lover to despair.

With feelings racked, without a spark
    Of hope to give those feelings rest,
The darksome grave is not so dark
    As is the chaos in his breast:
The brightest hour that comes and goes
    Might just as well be dull as bright,
His grief o'er all a shadow throws,
    That hides the splendour from his sight.

Unmoved he eyes the sun arise,
  Yea, doth without a thrill behold
The sun down go at ev'ning, tho'
  He settles in a sea of gold:
The sweetest flower of field or bower,
  The brightest star by night revealed,
To him's not rare, nor sweet, nor fair,
  For him no joyous beam can yield.

The tempest swells and roars and yells,
  Uptears and heaves to earth the oak;
The lightnings flash, the death-bolts crash,
  And cities wrap in flame and smoke:
Let thunder crash, and lightnings flash,
  And bid him perish as they can;
The storm he hears no death-dart bears
  Like that which makes his life a ban.

O'er all he sees, o'er all he hears,
  The raven shades of woe are cast;
And all his hopes, delights, and fears
  Are now but phantoms of the past;
The past, the present, future, ay,
  To all he's dead and cold, except
The worm that eats the heart away,
  Wherein yet Peace her vigils kept.

He wanders wide of human haunts,
  What others do he little recks ;
Their very sympathy or taunts
  Can little soothe, can little vex ;
Where'er he moves, where'er he turns,
  One, but one image meets his ken ;
For that he yearns and pines and mourns,
  And yearns and mourns for that in vain.

Away ! away with questions which
  No mortal yet could answer—nay,
My pangs are far beyond the pitch
  Of seraph-tongue or pen to say ;
To speak of love were but to speak
  Of what another might, whose heart
Was never forced like mine to break,
  Yet while it breaks to hide the smart !

The Broken Spell.

COME sing me the song that once gilded my gloom,
  And the heart unsubdued till that moment subdued,
That with its red rose caused the rose-tree to bloom,
  That long year after year without blossoms had stood.

With thy hand on my hand, and thy cheek by my cheek,
  In thy wild and weird tones be that lay again sung,
And the bleak world to me shall no longer be bleak,
  And this bosom by anguish no longer be wrung.

Then over thy grace shall thy voice throw a grace ;
  And that image which long had its home in my breast,
Be robed in a splendour no other displays,
  And possest of a charm by no other possest.

Than its red, shall thy lip then a richer dye show,
  And with beams brighter still shall thy hazel eyes burn ;
And thy beauty, deep down in my spirit, shall glow,
  And my life to a drop of pure ecstasy turn.

Shall the boon then be mine? shall that music reward
  Thus the faith of a heart that yet leapt at its strain?
Ah, broken's the spell of that song I oft heard,
  And so—so thro' thy dark guile to me shall remain !

Ah! canst thou forget?

A H! canst thou forget the hour when we met
 At the oak where the four lanes meet?
And madly I prest thy form to my breast,
 And my heart 'gainst thy heart did beat?

The moon hid her light in sorrow that night,
 While the owl in his grimmest mood
Cried "Whoo!" as I quaft in rapture a draught
 That a fiend for the nonce had brewed!

Lo! Never a Man.

LO! never a man since the world began,
　　Would bear what her victim hath borne;
And all he can gain for his toil and pain
　Is a look or a word of scorn.

She dances a tune that a hag would croon
　　When she erst o'er my pathway glanced;
And laughs in her sleeves at the heart she grieves;
　But she'll weep when the dance is danced!

In the Wild Grove.

IN the wild grove we wander'd,
  And gay garlands made,
When ill-wise we ponder'd
  On words in jest said.

And words, in jest spoken,
  The garlands we wove,
And our two hearts had broken,
  Ere we left the grove.

A Remembrance.

I STRAY 'neath a moon
  In a blood-red cloud ;
And my heart to a tune
  Is beating aloud—

Aloud to a tune,
  One, now in her shroud,
Sang to me 'neath a moon
  In a blood-red cloud.

No More Roses.

NO more roses ! He that's gone
    Was a star to look upon ;
And come weal or woe, yet one
    He'll so be to Dora !

Many women say of men,
Barely one is true in ten—
Who will he remember when
    He's away from Dora ?

When with blooms he wreathed my brow,
Made he not a certain vow ?
Will he think upon it, now
    He's afar from Dora ?

Fairer forms he'll see than mine ;
Eyes as black and yet more fine—
Will they not his heart incline
    To forget his Dora ?

What to think, I do not know ;
Yet I love and love him so,
In my hair no rose shall glow.
    Unplucked by him for Dora !

The Golden Bird.

I WILL not hear one cruel word,
   Or how he sinn'd, or how he err'd;
He's yet to me the golden bird
      He ever was to Dora !

I met him on the street to-day,
In haste to meet my rival gay ;
He turn'd from me his face away !
   —Yet, yet he's dear to Dora.

Into a floral shop he went,
I knew too well with what intent ;
Ah, not for me the wreath was meant !
   —Yet, yet he's dear to Dora.

While I sit here a weary wight,
He with my foe, to her delight,
Will dance his bridal dance to-night !
   —Yet, yet he's dear to Dora.

My heart is rent : he's sore to blame ;
Yet blame him not, or kindly blame ;
I cannot hear a word would shame
      The golden bird of Dora !

On Bardon Hill.

OH ! I think, think still, how, on Bardon Hill,
    He stood beneath a golden cloud ;
And bold as a hawk, with his head thrown back,
    A merry tune whistled aloud.

That hour on the height, in his blink so bright,
    Lo ! I marked not the sun go down ;
But felt to my cost that my heart was lost,
    And my peace with my heart had flown.

Stanzas.

THE hopes that allured me
   To cope with the worst,
At length have secured me
   The tortures accurst,
     Of fever and grief,
     And frenzy—in brief,
Ills—ills from which Death is the only relief.

But Titan-like lieth
   My soul in her chains—
Hourly she sigheth,
   The answer she gains,
     But adds night and day
     To pain and dismay—
'Tis the scream of the vulture—Despair at his prey!

Lo! the Day.

LO! the day begins to rise,
  And the shadows of the night,
Overtaken with súrprise,
  Blushing fly his presence bright;
Cease thy briny tears to flow,
  Not another murmur sigh;
Thine hath been the cup of woe,
  Now be thine the cup of joy.

Wakened by the voice of morn,
  See, the little urchin Mirth,
How she, laughing Care to scorn,
  Skippeth o'er the jocund earth;
Don, O, don thy best attire,
  Snatch, O, snatch this balm to pain,
Ere the beams of day retire,
  And thy night sets in again.

A Golden Lot.

IN the coal-pit, or the factory,
  I toil by night or day,
And still to the music of labour
  I lilt my heart-felt lay ;

I lilt my heart-felt lay—
  And the gloom of the deep, deep mine,
Or the din of the factory dieth away,
  And a Golden Lot is mine.

Life and Death.

OH, what is Life? A magic night
        In which we still to phantoms yield;
And what is Death, if not the light
    By which the real truth's reveal'd?

The Mysterious Rider.

UPON a steed he came with speed,
  The Day behind him breaking;
And still he sped when Day o'erhead
  Her last farewell was taking.

"Ah, whither fliest?—Name thy goal!"
  "The Dark from which I bounded!"
He spake and fled; and in my soul
  The voice night-long resounded.

All Night-Long.

ALL night-long I heard the blast,
    And the sea-birds as they pass'd
With a yell up from the granite-guarded shore,
    And the waves the fierce winds lash'd,
    As against the rocks they dash'd,
And whose roar the caverns answer'd with a roar!

    Long years since then have flown,
    But the bitter blast then blown,
And that roar upon the shore, and that wild yell
    Yet re-echo in my brain,
    And I sigh and sigh in vain
For the hopes to which their mad song proved a knell!

The Wounded Bird.

" WHY thus ever on the wing?
    Why those woful notes that bring
To the eyes of one and all a briny tear?
    Down into thy nest alight;
    Rest, and in the morning bright,
We'll yet hear from thee a carol sweet to hear!"

" Ah, an arrow's in my breast;
    And when I but touch my nest
I'm e'er deeper pain'd and wounded, and must fly
    And wail, and fly and wail,
    Till, lo, my pinions fail,
When adown into my nest I'll drop and die!"

The Collier Lad.

MY lad he is a Collier Lad,
   And ere the lark awakes,
He's up and away to spend the day
   Where daylight never breaks ;
But when at last the day has pass'd,
   Clean washed and cleanly clad,
He courts his Nell who loveth well
   Her handsome Collier Lad.

Chorus—There's not his match in smoky Shields ;
     Newcastle never had
      A lad more tight, more trim, nor bright
      Than is my Collier Lad.

Tho' doomed to labour under ground,
   A merry lad is he ;
And when a holiday comes round,
   He'll spend that day in glee ;
He'll tell his tale o'er a pint of ale,
   And crack his joke, and bad
Must be the heart who loveth not
   To hear the Collier Lad.

At bowling matches on the green
  He ever takes the lead,
For none can swing his arm and fling
  With such a pith and speed :
His bowl is seen to skim the green,
  And bound as if right glad
To hear the cry of victory
  Salute the Collier Lad.

When 'gainst the wall they play the ball,
  He's never known to lag,
But up and down he gars it bound,
  Till all his rivals fag ;
When deftly—lo ! he strikes a blow
  Which gars them all look sad,
And wonder how it came to pass
  They play'd the Collier Lad.

The quoits are out, the hobs are fix'd,
  The first round quoit he flings
Enrings the hob ; and lo ! the next
  The hob again enrings ;
And thus he'll play the summer day,
  The theme of those who gad ;
And youngsters shrink to bet their brass
  Against the Collier Lad.

When in the dance he doth advance,
  The rest all sigh to see
How he can spring and kick his heels,
  When they a-wearied be ;
Your one-two-three, with either knee
  He'll beat, and then, glee-mad,
A heel-o'er-head leap crowns the dance
  Danced by the Collier Lad.

Besides a will and pith and skill,
  My laddie owns a heart
That never once would suffer him
  To act a cruel part ;
That to the poor would ope the door
  To share the last he had ;
And many a secret blessing's pour'd
  Upon my Collier Lad.

He seldom goes to church, I own,
  And when he does, why then,
He with a leer will sit and hear,
  And doubt the holy men ;
This very much annoys my heart ;
  But soon as we are wed,
To please the priest, I'll do my best
  To tame my Collier Lad.

Dolly Dare.

THO' Lizzy's sweet and Polly's neat,
　　And Fanny she is fair,
In all our street there's none to meet
　　So blithe as Dolly Dare.

In doors and out she stirs about
　　As if she felt aware,
By labour glows more red the rose
　　That dowereth Dolly Dare.

She, knitting, will a ditty trill ;
　　And to an old, old air,
The needles bright dance left and right
　　Of sweet-tongued Dolly Dare.

The pots and mugs and pans and jugs
　　Into their places fare,
And clearer glow and dearer grow
　　When touched by Dolly Dare.

The bread she bakes, the beds she makes,
　　And up and down the stair
On tripping toe will dancing go
　　The tidy Dolly Dare.

9

To words of mirth she scours the hearth,
    While in his easy-chair
Old Robin lies and, smoking, eyes
    With pride his Dolly Dare.

Her pail to fill she'll to the rill,
    Or to the well, and there
Doth clearly see Truth's self, for she
    Therein sees Dolly Dare.

'Tis thus away she'll while the day,
    And then to me repair,
When envy smit the moments flit
    O'er me and Dolly Dare.

The Blackbird.

"OH, my wee, wee bonnibell,
 Do to me the riddle tell;
Say to whom pipes yon piper on the tree?
 And for what I'd like to know,
 Can his silver carol flow,
Save for what yet fills his little heart with glee?"

"Ah, your riddle, I'm afraid,
 Sir, may not to-night be read;
But a pebble for your cobble take—and go;
 Show me why no bird can sing
 When a wild hawk's on the wing?
This back, hobble back to-morrow night and show!"

—Now the sun has left the hill,
 And the blackbird's note so shrill
Sends a silver-ringing echo down the dell;
 Yet the golden pipe's unheard
 Of my own heart-witching bird;
And what whistler ever whistled half so well?

He avowed he'd meet me here,
 And he comes not, and I fear
That his pipe is not so golden after all;
 Hark!—ah, no!—Yes, hark!—I hear
 A sweet whistle, sweet and clear,
That no blackbird ever blew in bower or hall!

—Yes, a bird of wing may fly
To the apple of his eye ;
But how, if he's inclined a wee prank to play ?
What if wild-wing'd bird proceed
Just to wet his charming reed,
From a little crimson cherry on the way?

Ah, you've heard a cruel word?
La, no hornet's nest is stirr'd !
But out a bonny bee from its hive here flew ;
Where a sweeter wine you'll get
Now your golden reed to wet,
Than a whistler from a cherry ever drew !

—To draw water from the well
Down I went into the dell,
Just ere the yellow moon in the sky did glow,
When a blackbird's wily song
Won and kept my ear so long,
That my wee heart went a-maying to my woe !

Now I know what to do—
I a weary way pursue ;
Nor the plight of her pet can my dear Aunt tell ;
Yet somehow she lets me know
When I next for water go,
I'll not hear a blackbird whistle at the well !

Baloo.

BALOO, my sweet baby—the blossom !
  I dandle't till weary, and sigh,
With not a bare drop in my bosom
  To silence its pitiful cry.

And had he but thought of the trouble;
  And had he but thought on the pain :
Tho' green in the blade with the stubble,
  I'm fated to bleach on the plain.

Erewhile yet the lauded of many,
  A flower in the garden was I;
Denied now a kind word from any,
  A weed on the common I lie.

But let anguish thus my heart rend, and
  The briny tear thus my cheek lave ;
The longest lane yet has an end, and
  The weary sleep sound in the grave.

The Wind-Bag.

HE praised my eyes, so bright and black ;
  He praised my locks, so crisp and brown ;
My silence sweet—nor was he slack
  My smile to praise—to praise my frown.

From top to toe, me o'er and o'er,
  He praised till—tut ! I laugh'd outright ;
Against the wind-bag clash'd the door,
  And thro' the key-hole squealed " Good-Night ! "

The Curtsey.

SHE dropt a curtsey as she went,
  And look'd—no cloud e'er look'd so black ;
I half suspect the angel meant
  To put my heart upon the rack.

And yet not so. Did she not know,
  One year ago, by her disdain,
Too well this deed was done to need
  The least bit doing o'er again ?

The Posy-Gift.

1.

YOU quite mistake the sprite you chase—
 I'm of the under, not the upper
Order of the fairy race;
 And cannot go with you to supper.

" You silly elf, Titania's self
 Will "—Tut, be there ! My mirth she quenches;
And her stiff airs kick me downstairs
 To my dear kitchen cats and wenches.

2.

HA, ha ! last night I served you right;
 The kick I gave—tho' I was sorry
I gave it you—but come and view
 What will allay your wrath and worry.

" That posy gay? Well, I daresay—
 Who gave it you? A lady?" Truly !
" What lady, pray?" That I will say,
 When you have learned your manners duly.

3.

THESE gems of grace unutterable
     Were pull'd within her very bowers;
Smell, senseless villain! smell them, smell!
   Say didst thou ever smell such flowers?

"Such flowers?"—the fellow seized his hat—
   "Such flowers?" he answer'd in derision;
"Well, I've heard questions strange, but that—
   I'd better run for—a physician!"

4.

COME, pretty flowers, and drink my tears;
     'Tis well my better reason chided,
Or I had box'd the rascal's ears,
   That so the little dears derided!

My ruth, not ire, the wretch demands;
   The magic every cup adorning,
How could he feel?—saw he the hands
   That placed them into mine this morning?

5.

WHAT fancies throng into the mind,
  When one upon this posy gazeth;
The more I look, the more I find
  Some semblance that one quite amazeth.

"What semblance, man? to what? to whom?"
  Go, lack-a-brain, and sweep the stable;
A wooden head must not presume
  To chatter at the Muse's Table!

6.

ONE fancy kicks another's heel;
  But let us seize one while it trembles
In act to fly, and make't reveal
  Wherein each bloom her charms resembles.

These violets blue, not filled with dew,
  But with my tears—are not these weepers—
"What would you say? her eyes are grey,
  And never flash'd two merrier peepers!"

7.

ONCE more, sweet Muse, a fancy choose ;
 Seize by the heels that winged fellow,
And he'll declare how this her hair—
 " Her hair is brown, that broom is yellow ! "

Then that one try, I know he'll cry
 This bean-bloom's like her lips. " Sweet booby !
That runner's quite a scarlet bright,
 Thy lady's lips are very ruby."

8.

GO, Musie, go ! you like, I know,
 To throw a glamour o'er my vision ;
And I but want the truth to chant,
 And Truth shall do it with precision !

He'll not aver this rose-bloom's her,
 This lily-bell, he knows not whether,
But he will tell she's lily-bell
 And red, red rose-bloom, both together !

9.

THESE flowers that so reflect the Grace
    Of one who is the Queen of Graces !
I'll pop into my richest vase,
    Where I may watch their pretty faces.

And should a fly approach their lips,
    Then, Mercy, shield the little sinner ;
For if I catch him on the hips,
    He'll never need another dinner !

10.

ALL things of beauty seek to draw
    Unto themselves like things of beauty
In homage to an inner law,
    And which to own's their bounden duty.

So deems my nose—this beauteous nose !
    That out of love and admiration
So oft, before this wall-flower, bows,—
    Or homage yields to this carnation.

11.

COME, let me smell thee, lily-bell ;
　　Another smell, my silver lily !
And thou, sweet rose, come to my nose—
　　Ah, whence those feelings, soft and silly ?

She smell'd you so ? the lady ?　No ?
　　I know she did ; her charming nosy
Drew nectar up from every cup,
　　Before she handed me the posy !

12.

THESE lovely blooms, their rich perfumes
　　And many colours, rich and glorious,
My soul illume, o'er care and gloom
　　To move a king—a king victorious !

To me things seem, as in a stream,
　　Or on the person of my idol,
To wear a sheen before unseen,
　　E'en by the gifted bard of Rydal !

13.

BLIND as the wretch who mock'd my flowers;
   Or rather mock'd their well-won praises,
And swore what came from Eden-bowers
   Were only buttercups and daisies—

As blind was I till—till—A hare!
   The thought is off, nor can I win it
Back to—well, to—I declare
   This stave must end with nothing in it!

14.

O DEAR, dear, dear! what shall ensue?
   My only thoughts are off, that clearly
Might have express'd the praises due
   To one I prize, and prize so dearly!

The wine has vanished, and the lees
   To serve up these, would leave one undone,
Not of the flock of chick-a-dees,
   That chirrup to the folk of London.

15.

" HA, ha ! ola ! yet phantom led,
  You, with your capers high and airy,
Must kick your heels till, heels o'erhead,
  You're kick'd into this fine quandary !

" You banged me off with scorn and scoff,
  Then spurn'd the aid—the Muse romantic's—
Dame's bonny brow to crown, and now
  You pay the piper for your antics ! "

16.

' TIS quite a treat, as singer knows,
  To have to own one's fairly beaten,
And council's held among the crows
  To learn how soon one may be eaten.

The owl also—But, let that go,
  And ere, with patience all expended,
You cry Forbear ! let me declare
  This carol of the Posy ended.

The Silent Bird.

WHAT wonder if sad,
  Or silent my strain,
For what can be had
  From a bird in pain?

On a vanished day,
  On my thorny bush,
From my heart, the lay,
  A rillet would gush.

Then I piped, day-long,
  In shade or shine;
Ah, my life was a song,
  And that song divine!

From love, not duty,
  The music sprung;
And I sang of Earth's beauty,
  Her glory I sung:

Of the morning light,
  And the dying day,
—When heard a-right—
  Yet rang my lay:

Of the heath-clad hill,
  Of the primrose dell,
And the dancing rill,
  My song would swell;

Of the swan-haunted mere
  Wherein—spell-bound—
Would the daffodil peer,
  My song would sound;

Of the lily who'd yearn
  Day-long on the lake,
For the moon's return,
  Would my song awake;

Of each flower that blows;
  Of the bee that clung
To the mouth of the rose,
  I piped and sung!

And many who heard
  Were touch'd with the lay,
And blessed the bird,
  As they went their way.

Then a joy was born
  In the drooping heart
Of the weary and worn
  And woe-engirt:

Nay, my song had a spell
  To soothe the pain
And the trouble to quell
  Of the madden'd brain—

Then under the sway
  Of the heart-trill'd stave,
The giddy were gay,
  The gay were grave;

And fickle youth
  And uncouth mays,
Grew noble in truth,
  Or golden in grace;

Nor could evil plight
  Befall the young,
Who heard aright
  The song I sung!

So I bless'd and was blest
  Till, ah, by the thorn
'Gainst which it prest,
  My heart was torn!

Heart-bleeding, now sad
  Or silent my strain,
But what can be had
  From a bird in pain?

——

END OF SONGS AND LYRICS.

OTHER POEMS.

Other Poems.

Thistle and Nettle.

'TWAS on a night, with sleet and snow
  From out the north a tempest blew,
When Thistle gathered nerve to go
  The little Nettle's self to woo.

Within her father's cottage soon
  He found the ever-dreaded maid;
She then was knitting to a tune
  The wind upon the window played.

His errand known, she, with a frown,
  Up from the oaken table sprung,
Down took the broom and swept the room,
  While like a bell her clapper rung.

"Have I not seen enough to be
  Convinced for ever, soon or late,
The maid shall rue the moment she
  Attendeth to a wooer's prate?

"How long ago since Phemie Hay
  To Harry at the Mill fell wrong?
How long since Hall a prank did play
  On silly Nelly Brown?—how long?

"How long ago since Adam Smith
  Wooed Annie on the Moor, and left
The lassie with a stain? yea, with
  A heart of every hope bereft?

"But what need instance cases? lo!
  Have I not heard thee chaunt the lay,
'The fraud of men was ever so
  Since summer first was leafy?' eh?

"When men are to be trusted, then,
  —But never may that time befall;
Of five times five-and-twenty men,
  There's barely five are men at all.

"Before the timid maid they'll fall,
  And smile and weep and sigh and sue,
Till once they get her in their thrall,
  And then she's doomed her lot to rue.

"For her a subtle snare they weave,
  And when the bonny bird is caught,
Then, then they giggle in their sleeve;
  Then laugh to scorn the ill they've wrought.

"As other weary winds, they woo
  The bloom its treasures to unfold;
Extract its wealth—their way pursue,
  And leave her pining on the wold.

"When poppies fell like lilies smell,
　When cherries grow on brambles, when—
When grapes adorn the common thorn,
　Then women may have faith in men.

"Then may we hear what they may swear;
　Till then, sir, know I'm on my guard,
And he, the loon that brings me down,
　He, he'll be pardoned, on my word."

Thus for an hour her tongue was heard;
　By this, her words grown faint and few,
She raised the broom at every word,
　And thumped the floor to prove it true.

In ardent words the youth replied :—
　"Dread hollow-hearted guile thou must;
But deem not all of honour void,
　Nor punish all with thy mistrust.

"A few, not all, the lash have earn'd,
　Let but that few the lash assail;
The world were topsy-turvy turned,
　Did not some sense of right prevail.

"Destroy the weed, but spare the flower;
　Consume the chaff, but keep the grain;
Nor harry one who'd die before
　He'd give thy little finger pain."

On hearing this, she sat her down,
  Took up her needlework again,
And tho' she strove to wear a frown
  Made answer in a milder strain.

"Forego thy quest. Deceitful words
  May yet, as they have been, may be
A fatal lure to lighter birds ;
  They'll never prove the like to me.

"Still by my chastity I vow,
  As I have kept the cheat at bay,
So, should I keep my senses, so
  I'll keep him till my dying day.

"The best that man can do or say,
  The love of gold or rubies rare,—
Not all that wealth can furnish, may
  Once lure to leave me in a snare.

"So end thy quest." He only prest
  His ardent suit the more, while she
At every word he uttered, garr'd
  Her fleeing needles faster flee.

"My quest by honour's justified ;
  I long have eyed and found thee still
The maid I'd like to be my bride ;
  Would I could say the maid that will.

"Hadst thou but been a daffodil
    That with the breezes sport and play,
For all thy suitor valued, still
    Thou so hadst danced thy life away.

"But thou so fair art chaste." Thus he
    Unto her answer answers e'er,
And that too in a way that she
    Must will or nill his answer hear.

- And then a chair he'd ta'en, his chair
    Unto her side he nearer drew ;
Recurr'd to memories sweet and rare,
    And in a softer key did woo.

" Must all the passion which I've sought
    So long to hide be paid with scorn ?
A heart with pure affection fraught
    Be doomed a hopeless love to mourn ?

"And must thou still its homage spurn ?
    And must thou still my suit reject ?
And be to me this cruel thorn ?
    Reflect upon the past, reflect !

"A time there was, and time shall pass
    To me ere that forgotten be,
When side by side from tide to tide
    We played and sported on the lea.

"Ay, then have I not chased the bee
 From bloom to bloom—oft chased and caught,
And having drawn its sting in glee,
 To thee the little body brought?

"Then when a bloom of rarer dyes
 Into my busy fingers fell,
To whom was reached the lucky prize?
 Can not thy recollection tell?

"As oft away as summer went,
 Who pulled with thee the haw, bright, brown—
Brown as thy own bright eyes—and bent
 For thee the richest branches down?

"With blooms I've graced thy yellow hair,
 With berries filled thy lap, thy hand,—
That hand as alabaster fair,
 Had every gift at my command.

"Nay, tho' to others dour, yet meek
 I ever was to thee, and kind;
And when we played at hide-and-seek,
 I hid where thou would'st seek to find.

"Upon the playground still unmatched
 Was I, unless my loved one played;
And then it seem'd to those who watched
 My failures were on purpose made.

"As sure as e'er a race began,
   The palm was mine unless she joined,
And then I always was out-ran,
   For still with her I lagged behind.

"The ball I drove to others, mocked
   Their efforts to arrest its flight;
But when my ball to her was knocked,
   It would upon her lap alight.

"None, up and down so well I bobbed,
   To skip the rope with me would try;
Did she attempt? my skill was robbed;
   Another skipped her out—not I.

"At play thus was't; but childhood past,
   And ere the lasses reach their teens,
Atween them and the lads a vast
   Mysterious distance intervenes.

"They seldom on the green appear
   In careless sport and play; and if
They join the throng erect they wear
   Their head, and still their air is stiff—

"They all they know not what. And such
   The change that on my lassie fell;
Then would she shrink my hand to touch,
   And I half feared her touch as well.

"Had I changed too? This, I can tell,—
    That touch o'er me a spell would cast ;
And did I pass her in the dell,
    With slow and snail-like pace I pass'd.

"Her voice had lost its former ring,
    Yet, in that voice such power was flung,
I better liked to hear her sing,
    Than when of old to me she sung.

"Her touch, her tone, would make or mar
    My bliss, and tho' with all my skill
I strove to please, and please but her,
    I in her presence blundered still.

"When by the hearth she sewing sat,
    Did I to thread her needle try?
Still, still my heart played pit-a-pat,
    And still I miss'd the needle's eye.

"As with the needle-threading, so
    We with the skein a-winding fared,
And Auntie's dreaded tongue would go
    Before the dancing end appeared.

"'What ails the lass?' she often said—
    'She's sound asleep!' once said, and flew,
And snatched and snapt the tangled thread,
    While I—I know not how—withdrew.

"Away, too, fled those hours! Alack!
   They came and went like visions rare,
To mock the heart, delude and wrack,
   And leave the gazer in despair.

"Ah, less—tho' sun-illumed—less fair
   The blobs that dance adown the burn,
And let them burst they'll re-appear
   Ere those delightsome hours return.

"Yet they may live in thought, and could
   They live in Nettle's thought again,
Would she not change her bearing? would—
   Would she not change this bitter strain?

"Would she her lover still disdain?
   Would she continue thus to gall
And put him to this cruel pain?
   —Recall to mind the past, recall!"

Thus onward, on, his ditty flows,
   Until—her ruffled brow is sleek,—
Till, lo! the lily drives the rose,
   The rose the lily from her cheek.

And now the iron, sparkling hot,
   Around with might and main he swings,
And down upon the proper spot
   With bang on bang the hammer brings!

"O, be my suit but undenied,
　And, ere the moon is on the wane,
A knot shall by the priest be tied,
　The priest shall never loose again.

"In heart and hand excell'd by none,
　Henceforth I'd front the ills of life ;
And every victory I won
　Should be a jewel for my wife.

"So should the people of the dell,
　When they convened to gossip, say
For harmony we bore the bell,
　And bore it with a grace away.

"Nay, lift thy head, be not ashamed,
　If thus to feel—and thus, and—O !
As matters sinful might be blamed,
　Our saints were sinners long ago."

Deep silence here ensued.　The cat,
　That lately to the nook had crept
To mark the sequel of their chat,
　Came forth—lay on the hearth and slept.

The needles bright, that left and right,
　As if with elfish glee possest,
Had gleamed and glanced, and frisked and danced,
　In quiet on her apron rest.

In concert with the storm within,
  The storm without forbears to blow ;
And 'tween the sailing clouds, begin
  The joyous stars to come and go.

O'er all delight and silence brood,
  While to her wooer's bosom prest,
Poor Nettle's heart beats, beats aloud
  The tune that pleases lovers best.

And Thistle's pleased and Thistle's blest,
  And Thistle's is a joy supreme ;
Ay ! now of Nettle's smiles possest,
  He revels in a golden dream.

Dream on, brave youth :—An hour like this
  Annuls an age of cark and strife,
And turns into a drop of bliss
  The bitter cup of human life.

The tear is by a halo gilt,
  The thorns of life are turned to flowers,
The dirge into a merry lilt,
  When love returned for love is ours.

" I've heard," in language low and soft,
  Now Nettle's heart begins to flow ;—
" I've heard of honey'd tongues full oft,
  But never felt their force till now.

"Still would I fume, as day by day
　　I've seen the lasses bought and sold
By some I'd scorn'd to own, had they
　　Outweighed their very weight in gold.

"My hour of triumph's o'er.　In vain
　　Did I my fellow-maids abuse ;
I've snatched the cup, and drank the bane
　　Which sets me in their very shoes ;

"That turns a heart of adamant
　　To pliant wax ; and, in my turn,
Subjects me to the bitter taunt,
　　The vanquished victor's ever borne ;

"That leaveth Nettle satisfied
　　To leave her kith and kin, and by
Her ever-faithful Thistle's side,
　　To shelter till the day they die."

To W. R.

A Friend in Australia.

O WILY Willie Reay, I've read
    Your book of rhymes, and be it said
Few sweeter rhymes were ever made
        To grace our tongue
Since Burns, with Scotia's Muse's aid,
        His ditties sung.

The bonnie banks of Wanie's burn,
With Bothal's Castle, old and stern,
And fane revered where in an urn
        Of fame's yet shown,
Engage your charming muse in turn
        With scenes less known.

The coy bell-blooms in purple dark,—
Shade-loving mays that seem to hark
To what the skyward soaring lark
        May o'er them sing,—
You in the wood with pleasure mark
        Return each Spring.

Delighted, too, you see unclose
The petals of the pale primrose;
The sweetest flower that comes and goes,
        While—life to hear!
Yet down the glen the blackbird blows
        His whistle clear.

E'en so your heart dirls to behold
The little daisy's charms unfold,
As when with me in days of old,
      Its blooms among,
You heard the linnet's love-tale told
      In many a song.

O'er these and scenes like these you brood;
And when wrapt in a higher mood,
The aidance of the muse is sued,
      Then, then behold;
Their living pictures many-hued
      Your lines unfold.

Nor less to you than Wanie rare,
The banks of Wear, beyond compare,
For castles grand, whose towers yet wear
      The airs they wore,
When steel-girt enemies drew near,
      In days of yore.

There Lumley bold to Lambton shows
A front that almost threatens blows;
And Lambton up the valley throws
      A look at him,
With which her lords once answered foes
      In battle grim.

But scenes of war and war's alarms,
Proud prancing steeds and knights at arms,
And other founts of human harms,
      Ah, let us fly
To scenes of peace;—still, these have charms
      For you and I.

Away, away then let us steer
Our courses higher up the Wear,
To where old Finchale's ruins dear,
        For ages vast,
Have looked into the waters clear,
        That gurgle past.

Beneath yon trees once grim and stern—
Which seem in fancy's ken to yearn
For days that were when they would spurn
        And backward beat
The fiercest blast that blew—we'll turn
        And take a seat.

Upon the crispy fern we'll rest
And gaze upon the scene possest
Of what is sweetest, dearest, best,
        To souls like ours ;
The winding slopes in verdure drest—
        The trees and flowers.

Hard by in shade the foxglove dwells,
And rears on high her purple bells,
From which, when wind-a-dangled, wells
        In fancy's ear
An air no mortal air excels,
        Nor yet can peer.

There may one see the poppy burn
Amid the yet green waving corn ;
And when the yellow grain is shorn,
        We yet may see
This black-eyed crimson queen adorn
        In tufts the lea.

Blue-bottles too, whose tender hue
Will match the sky's own lovely blue,
Upon an early morn, we'll view,
   A pleasure rare:
But how can I describe to you
   What we'll see there?

There, there upon a holiday,
Will toilers in their best array,
Come with their little ones to play,
   A pleasant sight ;
And many a prank is played ere day
   Hath taken flight.

There, on some bonnie afternoon,
While bees awake a drowsy tune ;
Or, later on, while cushats croon
   A heartfelt lay,
And o'er them hangs the yellow moon,
   Will lovers stray.

In such an hour it were a treat
To hear our minstrel's self repeat
His May Morning, in accents meet ;
   That carol true,
And one more musical and sweet,
   I never knew.

The gift to warble such a song
Can but to Nature's bards belong,
With whom we'd rather dree the prong
   Of Want's grim self,
Than revel with you gilded throng
   That worship pelf.

Ah ! never crony let us fash
Our heads about a lot of cash ;
Nor seek with sparks to cut a dash ;
   Compared, I say,
What are the gauds they prize but trash
   To one sweet lay.

This, when away yon castles proud
Have vanished like some ragged cloud,
That nor'-land winds a-piping loud
   Have o'er them blown,
May yet to hearts by labour bowed
   A joy be known.

And such a lay let me aver
Will prove "May Morning" or I err ;
And "Jenny," too, tho' I prefer
   To this a third ;
E'en that wherein you curse the cur
   That shot the bird.

All these are very sweet and fine,
And to my palate, precious wine,
And every stanza, every line,
   As water clear,
Awakes a melody divine
   To charm the ear.

But end I must ; awhile adieu
To you and those so dear to you ;
And hinney, Willie, kiss them, do,
   Your bairns and wife,
In kind remembrance of your true,
   Fond friend for life.

The Rydal Trip.

D EAR Willy, now the March hath blown
     His last wild blast once more and flown,
And April, like my muse yet prone
        To change, comes in,
Again, to thee my rhyming crone,
        A rhyme I'd spin.

I'm brimming o'er with things to say,
Could I but only find the way
My thoughts and feelings to convey
        In language clear,
About a visit I did pay
        The Lakes last year.

Then up, Muse up, this task profound,
Up, up and do ! with bound on bound,
Away to England's Pleasure Ground,
        Away and ring,
And to thy Northern harp's wild sound,
        Its glories sing !

First on to sacred Grasmere—Why,
Why what a giddy goose am I,
Away before my tale to fly !
        On Rapture horsed,
We'll come to Grasmere by-and-by—
        But Keswick first !

From there we'll in the day-dawn go
And o'er the clear, cool Derwent row;
Then scale Lodore, tho' e'er so slow,
       Which having done,
Thro' Watendlith with mop and mow,
       To Rosthwaite run !

Next to the Druid Cirque we'll fare,
And dream an hour o'er days that were;
And dreams will often show more clear
       Life's issues than
The Daily Press from year to year
       Read daily can.

—The D. P.? La ! what wizen'd witch
Hath popt my nose into this ditch,
To smell the—pah !—the filth, the pitch
       With which the drab,
The pimp and lackey of the Rich,
       The Poor bedaub?

Help ! help me out of this ! then you
Sweet Elves may pinch me black and blue;
That's if you—Mercy !—how I rue—
       Help, help, and O !
Let's fly to Rydal as we flew
       One year ago !

To pitch and spite, cry we, Good Night !
Nor let Helvellyn in his might
Of magic to arrest one's flight,
       A counter count,
Ere we with love a-glow alight
       On Rydal Mount !

No sooner said than done : and there,
How wags the world, what need we care?
The men will at each other swear
      Till they are blue ;
The women tear each other's hair ;
      And let them ! Pooh !

Are all not born to err? and worse—
But you can tell them that, of course,
Not I—I'm but a man of verse
      That needeth bread,
And to put money in my purse
      I must be read.

"Lo! from what height on which agog
You rode, down thro' what dense, dark fog,
Into what deep Serbonian bog
      Have you been drawn,
Thus at Fate's feet a very dog
      To whine and fawn?

"Up, up, for shame, thou wretch! and let
Thy face against the False be set ;
Tho' harder lot be thine than yet
      Thou once hast known,
Up, up, and let in hues of jet
      The truth be shown !

"A bran new pen this moment grasp,
Not dipt in spue of toad or asp,
Not tipt with sting of critic-wasp,
      But in, with what
May thy thought-burdened heart unclasp"—
      To whom? "Whom not?

"To one and all show, show"—But then,
What needs this fuss about a pen
To picture to my fellow-men
      How very low
The masks in which they revel, when
      This truth they know?

'Tis not so much from lack of light
To know the wrong, to know the right,
Nor yet from lack of feeling quite,
      But want of will,
They chase the phantoms that delight
      To cheat them still.

Their brains with fancies frantic teem,
At which their eyes with rapture gleam;
They seek to grasp their idols—seem
      To grasp, anon,
To find each jewel but a dream—
      Yet they dream on.

Yet with a glamour o'er them, they
Still play to lose, yet losers play
A game which, won, would not repay
      A moment lost
Of but one golden summer day,
      Its winning cost.

Ah, what is worse, the spell that binds,
Oft saps the very best of minds,
Nor leaves its victim till he finds
      His love of all—
All good hath vanished with the winds,
      Beyond recall !

Then lo, the plight of such; henceforth
Their natures change; then real worth
Becomes to them a theme for mirth;
          While baubles small,
As oft in turn to praise give birth:
          —Nor is that all.

Not all that one might say, and would,
Had we been in the cue, and could;
Then we must on, and leave or should,
          This flowing fount
Of solemn thought—this neighbourhood
          Of Rydal Mount.

A holy something in the air,
Yet makes the merry Muse forbear
Her quips and cranks; an inner prayer,
          And thoughts of God,
Are mine, as I thro' pathways fare,
          That Wordsworth trod.

You little tinkling waterfall,
That scented flower upon the wall,
That doth the ear and eye enthrall,
          May once have warmed
And charmed a soul whose eye saw all,
          As mine is charmed.

Upon this very garden seat,
Where now I sit with feelings meet,
I see him sit in spirit sweet,
          With upward gaze,
And some grand song new-born repeat,
          With glowing face.

Where'er I turn, his form appears
In fancy's eyes ; in fancy's ears
One hears thy voice, enraptured hears,
   Thou great Song-child,
Upon whose hopes thro' long, lone years
   Thou mightst have smiled !

Thou mightst have grasped him by the hand,
And bid his heart with joy expand ;
Thou mightst his flame of song have fann'd,
   For thou wert strong
In human love, as thou wert grand
   And great in song.

Yea, as thy brother in renown,
That Prince of Song in London Town,
Just ere his sun of life went down,
   With thy regard
Thou mightst have stoopt this hour, to crown
   The rustic bard.

Like him to—me ?—In every limb,
I shake—I shake !—My senses swim—
What did I say ? Thou memory grim,
   What hast thou done ?
Was ever bard, to me, like him
   Beneath the sun ?

Ah, why recall that moment, why,
That only came, anon, to fly
Before a day so dark ?—I sigh—
   While I have breath,
I'll mourn the wrench I suffered by
   Rossetti's death !

"And yet, fond heart, no vain regret ;
Our path's not all by thorns beset ;
We mourn the lily vanished, yet
   Oft fail to prize
Some little golden violet
   Before our eyes.

"And with such boons thrice-blest art thou—
And woe betide the black-wind, woe !
Would turn, or lay their sweet heads low,
   And so away
Its glory and its perfume blow
   From thy life's day !

" Oft in the coal-pit's murky gloom
Would come that glory and perfume,
To cheer thee, sweeten, and illume,
   What else had ne'er
Been other than a cruel doom
   For bard to bear.

"With music sweeter than the trill
Of warbling bird, or gurgling rill,
Will memories dear the heart-strings thrill,
   Or soon or late ;
And thine are such, and will be still,
   In spite of Fate !"

But this, of this, too much, and now
To Rydal we will make our bow,
" From Rydal you're afar, sir, now—
   Down, you came down
So swift—Ah, slipt you not somehow,
   And crack'd your crown ?"

I crack'd my—— Well, of this we'll crack
As we to Coaly Tyne go back;
And not to hold you on the rack,
   One look we'll throw
At Windermere, pack up, off pack,
   And back we'll go.

—The more the haste the less the speed,
As sang the tailor to his thread;
And this we'd find in very deed,
   Unto our woe,
Did we to Memory give heed;
   But—back we'll go.

"Come, come," she cries, "and I will show
You sights will charm your senses so;
Scolfell the huge and Silverhow,
   And"—But our track
Is backward bent, and back we'll go;
   Yes, we'll go back!

"A passing blink you'll not refuse
To Hunting Stile at least; nor choose
But yield the grace and worth one views
   Thereat"—Just so;
Now would this charmer charm the Muse;
   But—back we'll go!

Yes, we'll go back; yet had we power,
A song would be yon lady's dower,
As sweet as e'er in midnight hour,
   To bugle-ring,
Did Echo from her airy tower
   In rapture sing!

Ay, could the deed the will display,
Then, then were sung what thou, mad fay,
Sweet Echo, to its spells a prey,
   Would yet prolong,
Till all the world had pass'd away
   In one´wild song !

So would we, could we ; but between
This would and could doth intervene
A gulph, from which the Muse in teen
   Must turn and—O !
That sudden jerk ! What can it mean?
   Where are we now?

"By Coaly Tyne, sir, and 'tis plain
Not on a hack, but in a Train,
Which you must out !" Well, I've a brain !
   —Well, I may Work
Myself into myself again
   Thro' that same jerk.

Meanwhile, my friend, for heart and fun
Unmatched, Good Night ! Our task is done ;
The Muse is off—her rhyme is spun—
   Her zig-zag flight
Has ended where it was begun—
   Good Night ! Good Night !

To W. R.

A Friend in Australia.

TO you, on you, my Willy Reay,
  To you, on you, so many a day,
Out o'er the seas and far away,—
        A word or two,
A wee to ease my heart, I'd say
        A word on you.

In this my wifie's thought's express'd,
For well I know within her breast
She ranks you with the truest, best
        Of friends that I
Possess, or ever yet possest
        In days gone by.

We've had our troubles great and small
Since last we met you, but 'mid all
We've thought of you and yours, and shall,
        While life endures,
With rapture sweet the names recall
        Of you and yours.

And often in the night-tide hours,
When, toil-relieved, and memory pours
Into our souls her sweetest showers,
        Her healing dew,
Distilled from joy and sorrow's flowers,
        We'll talk of you.

Of all the funny tales you'd tell
About the folks upon the Fell,
Where Teams flows onward yet to swell
          Our own dear Tyne,
We'll talk as if beneath a spell
          Almost divine.

The twinkle of your eye when aught
Grotesque or sweet your fancy caught,
And ended in some happy thought,
          Or feeling deep ;
Of this with painful pleasure fraught,
          We'll talk and weep.

Your jokes that never left a sting,
Of your bright laugh, whose merry ring
Told of the pureness of its spring,
          The hours away,
We'll talk, talk, talk of every thing
          You'd do or say.

Nor only of the joys that were,
But what the golden hour will bear
When you return, we'll talk ; for ne'er,
          Befall what may,
Can we of your return despair,
          Nay, never ! nay.

That cruel thought we could not dree,
That cruel thought we'll flee and flee,
Till you again have cross'd the sea ;
          For come you will,
And with your heart-inspiring glee,
          Our feelings thrill.

Then will we mock at curst mischance,
And sing our song and dance our dance ;
And on our native hobbies prance,
   Unlike yon crew
Who merely ape the apes of France
   In all they do.

A little fun will oft engage
The moments of the deepest sage ;
And tho' we're somewhat touched with age,
   Our jokes we'll crack,—
Nay, Glee on Care a war will wage
   When you come back.

As wont, we'll ramble up and down
Our smoky and yet rare old town ;
Most rare I say, and with a frown—
   What ! Willy, what !
Would we not face a king or clown,
   Would say it's not?

We'll down and see the castle grand,
So firmly built, so nobly planned ;
And at whose feet two bridges stand,
   Of rare design,
By which from bank to bank is spann'd,
   Our Coaly Tyne.

We'll see St. Nicholas as of old,
For beauty worth its weight in gold,
Nor heed if others suns behold,
   In fanes afar,
To which compared our own, we're told,
   Is but a star.

12

Confound the carpers who compare
The virtues of our jewels fair,
As if they loved away to scare
            Some vision which
Might otherwise with magic rare
            Our lives enrich !

Have we not ills enough and more,
But we must keep a bolted door,
Lest some stray fay from Beauty's shore,
            Of Love begot,
Glide in to charm us evermore?
            La ! have we not ?

But whither flies the Muse? A throng
Of feelings hurries her along ;
Yet like the tinkler in the song,
            In all her flight,
Just when she seems to go most wrong,
            She goes most right !

Your nags so hide-bound, stiff, and tough,
May suit old hags, gaunt, grim, and gruff,
But not the gipsy elves, enough,
            Whose spirits high
Would into airy nothing puff
            The world they fly !

On winged steeds they'd go ; nor will
Our Muse less swift scour onward still,
When thrill our heart-strings as they thrill,
            Nay, almost crack,
At thought of how the time we'll kill
            When you come back !

We'll then, as I have said and say,
The glories of our town survey;
A visit to the Dene we'll pay;
        Then down the burn
We'll link ho! ho! we'll link that day,
        When you return.

Away to canny Shields will we,
And bonny Whitley-by-the-Sea,
Then up to Hexham in our glee;
        Nay, rest we'll spurn
Till all the country-side we see,
        When you return.

That will we view, and many a thing
To which our sweetest feelings cling,
And from our harps shall flow a spring
        From rapture born,
That many a lad and lass shall sing,
        When you return.

When you return; when Mary Jane
And you come sailing o'er the main,
No storm will blow the ship to strain—
        Each charm-bound wave
Will duck its head down till you gain
        Our harbour safe.

That day of days?—Run, Sally, run!
And stop the tune in love begun,
Or I shall harp till I'm undone,
        And have, alack!
No strength to hug our cronies, none!
        When they come back.

Not, not so fast. Ah, there, now there,
You've bumped your chin against the chair
And bit your tongue—well I declare !
   That tongue that's rung
Me many a curtain song so rare,
   Since we were young.

" Ha, ha ! " you cry: well, darling, well,
I'm glad that naught occurr'd to quell
The music of that golden bell,
   And that its clack
May help my welcome cry to swell
   When Will comes back.

Till then, again, adieu, my friend,
And when you have an hour to spend
On rhyme, a rhyme thy crony send :
   Do, Willy do ;
Meanwhile, believe me to the end,
   A brother true.

THE END.

THE WALTER SCOTT PRESS, NEWCASTLE-ON-TYNE

Carols, Songs, and Ballads,

By JOSEPH SKIPSEY.

" The whole book deserves to be read, and much of it deserves to be loved. . . . As for the qualities of his poetry, they are its directness and its natural grace. He has an intellectual as well as metrical affinity with Blake, and possesses something of Blake's marvellous power of making simple things seem strange to us, and strange things seem simple. How delightful, for instance, is this little poem ! . . . How exquisite and fanciful this stray lyric ! . . . We admit that Mr. Skipsey's work is extremely unequal, but when it is at its best it is full of sweetness and strength ; and though he has carefully studied the artistic capabilities of language, he never makes his form formal by over-polishing. Beauty with him seems to be an unconscious result rather than a conscious aim ; his style has all the delicate charm of chance. . . . We have already pointed out his affinity to Blake, but with Burns also he may be said to have a spiritual kinship, and in the songs of the Northumbrian miner we meet with something of the Ayrshire peasant's wild gaiety and mad humour. He gives himself up freely to his impressions, and there is a fine careless rapture in his laughter. . . . Mr. Skipsey can find music for every mood, whether he is dealing with the real experiences of the pitman, or with the imaginative experiences of the poet, and his verse has a rich vitality about it. In these latter days of shallow rhymers it is pleasant to come across some one to whom poetry is a passion, not a profession."—*Pall Mall Gazette*, Feb. 1, 1887.

"Mr. Skipsey is always original. The echoes of any former poets are few and faint. Blake, perhaps, oftener than any other, is suggested ; for example, in 'The Moth,' or in the graceful verses named 'The Violet and the Rose.' . . . There may be a suggestion of Blake in these lines ; but certainly there is no imitation. . . . Mr. Skipsey's range is a very wide one. He passes easily from grave to gay, from lively to severe. . . . He has his hours of depression, and can sing. . . . But his wonted attitude is one of aspiration and hope. . . . Shakepeare need not have been ashamed if he had written this song."—*The Academy*, January 22, 1887.

"Bright with many a flash of genuine poetry."—*Glasgow Herald*.

"He has humour, pathos, imagination, and a kind of unaffected veracity. Perhaps his 'Collier Lad' is the most effective and popular of his pieces, but his 'Arachne' shows fancy in a very different class of work.   Contrast this with the miner's ditty, 'Get up.' . . . Is not that good and manly and natural?   It is as terse as an epigram from the Greek anthology.   Mr. Skipsey has a very great width of range.   His love poems are extremely touching and earnest. . . . Like the minstrel in the *Odysseus*, he might probably say, 'Self-taught am I, and the God puts all manner of songs into my heart,' whence they spring again in ringing measures, worth many volumes of cultivated and decorated verse."—*Daily News*, December 17, 1886.

"In healthy, homely sentiment, and often, too, in lyrical quality, his lyrics remind us of Robert Burns. . . . They go straight from heart to heart."—*Scotsman.*

"Mr. Skipsey is decidedly at his best in such poems as 'Mother Wept,' 'My Little Boy,' 'Tit-for-Tat,' 'Life and Death,' and 'Willy and Jimmy'; the last named we cannot forbear quoting. . . Many of the shorter poems have a delicacy of imagery and subtle romanticism which remind us of Heine, for example, 'Annie Lee,' 'The Three Maidens,' 'The Fatal Errand,' 'Stanzas,' and 'Lo, the Day,' while often a deeper chord is struck by such a verse as the following . . . and true to the life is his portrait of the collier-lad."—*The Mining Journal*, March 8, 1887.

"There is enough of natural spontaneity and vigour to interest and charm.   Some of the ballads and lyrics have a pleasing air of unaffected homeliness, and are free from imitative trick or dexterity."—*Saturday Review*, November 1886.

"Mr. Skipsey has produced a volume of genuine poetry of such sweetness and dignified simplicity, spontaneity, and directness, as are rare in Literature."—*Birmingham Daily Post.*

"There is a happiness of execution in verses like this which our poets seem to have lost for some generations past.   Suckling had it, and Lovelace had it.   But the genius for this kind of work is altogether exceptional and of rare occurrence, a happy simplicity being indeed among the most scarce of poetic gifts.   In Mr. Skipsey's volume, however, we are continually encountering such delicate passages, as sparkling as the drops of rain upon the leaves of a wild brier."—*Shields Daily Gazette*, July 16, 1887.

"The real life pieces are more sustained and decided than almost anything of the same class I know.   I mean in poetry coming really from a poet of the people, who describes what he knows and mixes in. . . . 'Thistle and Nettle' shows the most varied power of all, perhaps. Other favourites of mine are 'Persecuted' [Cruel Annie], 'Willy to Lily,' 'Mother Wept' (this very sterling), the image evolved at page 25 [Alas, the Woe !], and 'Nanny to Bessy.' 'The Violet and the Rose' I think very perfect, and 'Get up' seems to me equal to anything in the language for direct and quiet pathetic force."—DANTE G. ROSSETTI, October 29, 1878, on *A Book of Lyrics.*

www.ingramcontent.com/pod-product-compliance
Lightning Source LLC
Chambersburg PA
CBHW031108020726
47495CB00007B/2105